God's Daughters and their Almost Happily Ever Afters

A Novel

Rita Roberts-Turner

ISBN 978-0-9964996-0-6
Library of Congress Control Number: 2015909391

Rita Roberts-Turner momturner@comcast.net

Editing by Cara Highsmith, Highsmith Creative Services, www.highsmithcreative.com

Cover and Interior Design by Mitchell Shea, www.atdawndesigns.com

Printed in the United States of America
First Edition 14 13 12 11 10 / 10 9 8 7 6 5 4 3 2 1

Nashville, TN

God's Daughters and Their Almost Happily Ever Afters

Chapter 1

Lena set a huge plate of food down in front of her husband. Eggs, fried potatoes, bacon, and biscuits. It was always too much, but he never said so. She slathered his biscuits with butter and jelly and stood waiting to refresh his coffee after each sip he took. He had turned the newspaper to his favorite section and his attention was fixed on the page.

Usually, she sat quietly, not eating anything herself, content to watch him eat. Today, he could feel her eagerness to interrupt his meal as she wiped over a spot on the table for the third time.

"What's up baby?" he finally asked between bites. He placed his hand on hers. She put down the dishrag and sheepishly gave him a broad grin.

"Guess what?"

"What?" he asked, mimicking her childlike playfulness.

"The First Ladies Society accepted my application and has invited me to go through its membership screening process," she said in one quick breath.

Her announcement was met with silence.

"I got the letter yesterday. Look," she said, pulling the letter from her pocket then sliding it and her chair closer to him. "Congratulations on your rise to becoming first lady of a *mega* church," she read aloud, not giving him a chance to read it for himself. "We're a mega church!" she squealed.

Pastor Richard wiped his mouth and hesitantly glanced over the letter. "It says we're on our way to *becoming* a mega church. We're not there yet. Why didn't you tell me you were applying?"

"I didn't want to jinx it, and I didn't get the official invitation call until last night." She could have reminded him that he wasn't home last night for her to share her news, but she decided not to taint her celebration with negativity.

"We should have discussed this," he said.

"Nothing's confirmed yet," she said, her voice dropping.

Richard had heard about the group's confirmation procedures and it made him uneasy—weeks of unannounced Sunday visits to the church, endless scrutiny of the ministerial background, and mandatory church financial disclosures. He didn't need the intrusion right now. Lena looked wounded, like a child who'd been told there is no Santa Clause. He knew she wouldn't join if he objected. He also knew he wouldn't be able to stand watching her disappointment. He'd caused her enough lately.

"Well you're going to be the finest first lady up in the place," he said playfully, trying to sound happy for her.

A slow smile stretched across her face as she threw her arms around his neck. "Thank you honey. This really is major you know. Everybody who is anybody in the church community belongs to this organization. Think of what this can do for the church... for you... for us!"

She gave Richard a long warm kiss on the lips.

"I'm so proud of you," she said sweetly.

He listened to her humming as she ran up the stairs. He wouldn't have been able to pretend with most women, but Lena was easy. Too easy. At that moment he wished she were stronger—the kind of woman he could share *everything* with.

Spring marked the beginning of another session of activity for the Christian First Ladies Society. FLS, as it had come to be known, only met from April to December (after Easter and before Christmas), but their projects kept them in the spotlight year round. In just five years their chapter of the organization had opened food banks across the city, bought and renovated houses for homeless families, and provided full college scholarships to ten local high school students. Through their husbands' churches, they had a reach of over 30,000 people, and the number doubled when you included the statewide members. That audience gave them the kind of influence local politicians and business leaders didn't dare ignore. When FLS needed something, FLS got it. Now, the ladies were ready to expand their influence throughout the country. This year's roster of invitees was the largest ever and they were looking for women with the leadership potential to form and maintain new chapters.

A parade of perfectly tailored pastel suits and ornate oversized hats buzzed around the meeting hall. The bigger the hat, the more esteemed the first lady. The FLS president had one of the biggest. Her face was barely visible under the wide, pink brim trimmed with white beads and flowers. As president, every meeting was held at her husband's church. The women carried on meaningless chatter and conspicuously inspected the more modestly dressed candidates who sat otherwise unacknowledged until the large grandfather clock in the corner of the room announced that it was noon. The Secretary tapped on her crystal goblet, summoning everyone to their seats. The meeting came to order with prayer, a hymn, and an impassioned reminder from the leadership to display unity, sisterly love, and respect. Candidate introductions came last.

There were twenty in all. Many were housewives with masters or doctorate degrees and nowhere to use them. Each year there was an unspoken movement to recruit more professional women, and each year the move was quashed by the "senior ladies," muttering objections such as:

"I just don't see how any woman who spends more time at the office than she does at the church and taking care of her family, could possibly be a good pastor's wife, let alone an FLS member."

These senior ladies had earned the privilege of attending only one meeting each year—the annual vote—and they used that privilege to continue steering FLS in the direction they felt it should go.

Few of the women were surprised by their invitation. They fully expected to be members one day, although they weren't foolish enough to say so out loud. Lena was different. She sat between Connie and Aliyah— her mentors, according to the nameplates at the table. She felt out of place surrounded by the elegant women whose every move she followed to make sure she grabbed the right glass and silverware. As the candidates introduced themselves, she rehearsed in her head what she would say when it was her turn and prayed she wouldn't mess up. Her nervousness was growing. Maybe she'd misread the letter. Maybe she wasn't even supposed to be there. Maybe this was a cruel joke she didn't get.

When she finally heard her name, she was so excited that she almost knocked over a glass of water. She caught it just in time as it tipped toward Connie, gave a gracious smile, and waved before sitting down. She was thankful she didn't have to speak, certain her words would have gotten twisted in her head before tumbling out of her mouth.

"And this concludes our opening meeting," the President announced as she slammed a gavel down on a small wooden board. The ladies joined hands, bowed their heads for one final prayer, and then descended upon the candidates.

"Study these. Learn these. Become these," Connie said, shoving mountains of material at Lena and two other candidates who had gathered around her. Usually she only had one candidate to deal with, but with this incoming class, she had three to oversee. She wasn't interested in getting to know any of them. Her only concern was getting them prepared for membership and making sure they didn't make her look bad in the process.

Lena was the first candidate Aliyah had coached, and she agreed to accept only one. Besides taking orders from Connie, who was the primary mentor, Aliyah wasn't sure what her job was supposed to be. Although a relatively new member herself, as the daughter of a founding member she knew everyone in the room. But, there was no one she'd really call a friend; FLS was simply mandatory for her.

"You set the example for the women in your church. They should want to emulate you—to be you," Connie said, sounding rehearsed. "You are the queen of your congregation."

Lena and the others nodded. Aliyah let out a tired sigh.

"And by the way, we are not nuns," Connie said, giving Aliyah a disapproving look. Aliyah had forced herself to come and had not dressed to impress. She wore a long floral dress that hung like a tent over a body she hated, and a stiff, white straw hat with a yellow ribbon was perched on her head like a basket covering the soft brown bundle of hair she didn't have time to curl. Someone surely would be on the telephone by the end of the day discussing her appearance with her mother.

The candidates were handed copies of rules and by-laws and their mentors' telephone numbers.

"Use these phone numbers sparingly," Connie chastised.

"Please," Aliyah more politely concurred.

Lena waited for more instructions. When none came she finally spoke.

"Would you ladies be interested in having lunch at

my house next week?" she asked, seemingly oblivious to or unimpressed by everything they had just heaped on her. Really, she was too scared to think about it.

Connie and Aliyah looked at each other, and then at Lena. The other two candidates also looked disapprovingly at Lena. Everyone knew you allowed your mentors to reach out to you first and not vice versa. They almost felt embarrassed for her.

"We'll call you," they said in unison without even a hint of enthusiasm.

Lena strummed her fingers across her husband's desk and gazed at their wedding picture standing alone on a dust-covered bookshelf. The simplicity of her cream ankle-length dress and his gray off-the-rack suit made her smile along with the memory of the first time she saw him when he walked into her high school English class and stretched out his long lean legs at the desk beside her. She was tucked away in the corner, unnoticed by pretty much everyone. He leaned over and asked, "What's a fine thing like you doing in the back of the room?" He was the first boy ever to call her beautiful, the first to hold her hand, and the only one she'd ever kissed.

She'd been waiting for thirty minutes in his office, which was really nothing more than an oversized supply closet. When she arrived at the church, eager to tell him all about her FLS meeting, he kissed her on the cheek, told her to wait, and darted off to the construction area with the contractors.

The new sanctuary was a massive structure that was taking over the dead end lot where the original church still stood. The first piece of ground had been turned over three months ago, and from the tiny window by his desk she watched Pastor Richard rattle on with the contractors and church trustees who trailed him as he wound his way through the partially exposed building. It was the largest building project in the church's fifty-year history and a refreshing sight for this rather blighted part of the city. The grand unveiling was next Sunday and Lena wasn't surprised when she saw the local television station pull onto the gravel lot. If she stayed, her job would be to sit and smile admiringly at him while he was peppered with softball questions. It wouldn't be hard. She did love and admire him. She was proud of what he was doing to turn the neighborhood around. But today, she wanted to tell him about her day.

She picked up her purse and walked out. Pastor Richard was standing at the curb greeting the reporter. He waved his arms in the air, pointing out his vision for each corner of the parking lot. He didn't see Lena when she got in the car and drove away.

Dinner was ready at six. She always had it ready by then, just as her mother and grandmother taught her, even though everything usually got cold before Pastor Richard made it home. She felt bad about not staying with him for the interview and she hoped he wasn't mad. She made his favorite foods—smothered pork chops, sweet potatoes, and collard greens—and was surprised to hear the door click just as she was putting the rolls on the table.

"You're home!" she said and threw her arms around his neck. "I made your favorites. It's all hot. Sit down and eat. And you'll never guess who is my mentor for FLS! Connie Jenkins. Yes! Connie Jenkins the television personality!" she said in one big breath before he could interrupt her. She fumbled for matches to light the candles she'd put on the table to remind him it was a special night. "All the women are so pretty, and we had a really fancy lunch. I've got so much to learn, but it's going to be really fun I think."

"That's nice baby," he said, still standing and holding a small pink bag.

"Is that for me?" she asked as she blew out the match she was holding before the flame reached her fingertips.

He nodded and handed her the bag. Inside was a small, heart-shaped container filled with jellybeans. She loved jellybeans and every year since they'd been married he brought her some for their anniversary. She smiled and leaned in to kiss him. She stopped when she felt him step back.

"I have to meet the bankers at the church in about an hour. I just came home to get some papers," he said hesitantly. "I'll take you out for a nice dinner this weekend."

Her hand squeezed tightly around the bag of jellybeans. As she stood and looked at him and all the food she'd cooked, she bit her lip. She tasted a tinge of blood.

Pastor Richard went upstairs before she could say anything. He knew she was hurt, but she'd get over it. Everything would be finished soon and things could get back to normal, at least that's what he kept telling himself.

Chapter 2

"Thank you God" was the last thing Aliyah's father said before collapsing in the pulpit. Stunned, silent grief permeated the church as the coroner rolled away his body. Church members huddled together weeping, shaking their heads in disbelief while the elderly churchwomen gathered around Aliyah's mother fanning and trying to calm her. In the frenzy, Aliyah's husband, the Reverend, barked orders to the deacons as he rushed out behind the coroner, leaving Aliyah sitting on the steps of the altar where her father's body had been stretched out while someone unsuccessfully tried CPR. With her arms folded tightly around her shoulders, she rocked back and forth, crying and trying to ignore the shooting pains that were cutting through her lower back.

"Oh God not now! Not now!" she gritted through her teeth.

Aliyah labored alone for six hours. The Reverend, who was busy making sure her father's death was properly announced, finally came after the doctor told him she was headed to surgery. Jeremiah entered the world via C-section weighing almost nine pounds.

Aliyah's mother hadn't found the strength to come. Shortly after the doctor declared it was a boy, the Reverend counted all of his fingers and toes, had the nurse snap a photo of him with the baby cradled in his arms, and then he headed back to the church. Aliyah didn't feel like holding Jeremiah and had the nurse take him back to the nursery. She wasn't even sure she'd looked at his face.

The hospital room was dark and still. A nurse was kneading her hands into Aliyah's abdomen and she felt as though her insides were being turned inside out.

"We have to make sure there are no clots," the nurse said mercilessly. "Tomorrow you'll get up and walk."

When she left, Aliyah buried her head into her pillow and cried until she began to shake uncontrollably.

The next morning the nurse brought Jeremiah into the room and tried to coax Aliyah into nursing. She declined and readily let the visitors who were coming every hour on the hour to pass him around and feed him. Her mother finally came too, her eyes puffy and swollen.

"He's perfect, just perfect," she sniffed, trying to fight back tears. "Your father would be so proud."

Flowers had been arriving all morning and the church secretary delivered a stack of cards. Aliyah fiddled with the mail and opened some of the cards stacked on her tray table. Most of them offered condolences rather than congratulations. At the bottom of the pile was a large Federal Express envelop that had been sent overnight. Inside was a simple post card with no return address:

> *I'm really sorry to hear about your dad.*
> *You're always in my thoughts.*
>
> *Love,*
> *Jay*

After all this time, Jay had found her. Of all times, when she couldn't be more unavailable, he was thinking about her. She wanted to ball up the card and throw it in the trash.

Aliyah cried every day. Sometimes for her father. Other days she didn't know why she was crying, but every day it seemed like a dark cloud hung heavy over her shoulder waiting to drop the weight of the world on her. She wanted to be like those women in the magazines, lovingly cuddling their newborns. But usually she just felt hollow.

A few months ago she was sure there would be nothing better than to touch, smell, and hold Jeremiah. She and the Reverend had wanted a baby so badly. They tried for two years before they finally saw a specialist. When the doctor couldn't find anything wrong, the Reverend suggested they start praying. And that's what they did. Every night they prayed and asked God to touch their bodies and bless them with a child they would gladly dedicate to Him. It only took six weeks before she was running to the bathroom in the middle of the night to cradle the toilet.

She was happy then, as happy as she could be. At night, the Reverend would lie in bed with her and rub lotion on her itchy, ballooning belly. They laughed and talked about diaper changes, late night feedings, and mandatory date nights with or without the baby. So far nothing had turned out as she planned.

"Your dad is in a better place," Pastor said, making an ill attempt to comfort her when he found her lying despondently on the couch every afternoon when he returned from the church.

"One life has passed, but you should be rejoicing and celebrating this new life God has given us," he told her, not that he had found the time to be around to help her with this new life. There had been an emergency vote by the congregation and he'd ascended to her father's position as head Pastor just a week after they'd laid him to rest. She despised the fact that the church was moving so quickly, as though her father hadn't existed. She almost hated looking at her husband some days when he came home.

Her mother had grieved severely, but after two weeks even she admonished Aliyah to, "snap out of this blue funk and get on with the business of being a mother." No one cared about or heard her silent screams.

Aliyah rested her head against the soft leather seat. The humming engine echoed in the garage, and she inhaled and waited. *It shouldn't take long,* she thought.

Jeremiah sat beside her in his car seat, asleep. She shouldn't take him with her. But what else could she do. The Reverend couldn't—wouldn't— take care of him the way he deserved.

This was the best way. No mess. No noise. Just sleep. That's all she wanted. God couldn't be mad about that; after all, He was the reason she was in this place. He took her father. He took away Jay—her one true love. She'd been praying for six weeks and He'd failed to even restore an ounce of her joy that He'd stripped away.

She swallowed hard and felt the sting of salty tears running down her cheeks. *It shouldn't take long,* she repeated to herself, interrupted by Jeremiah's sudden spasm of hiccups that woke him. Instead of crying, he kicked his legs and giggled through a mouth full of spit bubbles, delighted by this newly discovered movement. Aliyah watched him; his toothless, open-mouthed grin demanded nothing and everything of her.

She scooped him out of the seat, rubbed her chin against his soft curls and held him against her chest. His tiny hand gripped the side of her shoulder and his short easy breaths synchronized with hers. She turned off the car engine. Maybe God hadn't completely forsaken her.

Dinner was like a slow moving wake that you wanted to end even though what was ahead was no happier. Aliyah and the Reverend ate in silence, their eyes glued to their plates, afraid eye contact might demand conversation. The Reverend finished his food in a few swift bites and excused himself from the table to retreat to his books. Aliyah sat alone in the kitchen finishing her meal with Jeremiah. He had grown so much and was developing a little personality. She saw traces of her father in him when he laughed. When she thought about that night, several months ago in the car locked in the garage, she was thankful she had not done the unthinkable.

She surveyed the pile of dishes in the sink, leftovers surrounding the stovetop, and the baby covered in pureed peaches—all waiting for her. The muscles in her chest tightened as she exhaled deeply. She pulled Jeremiah out of his high chair and toted him into the living room.

The Reverend didn't look up. He was too focused on his sermon. It was already Friday and, for now, his Sunday sermon was little more than a few words on the page. He scribbled and erased almost simultaneously, clearly frustrated that his thoughts weren't coming together. Aliyah put Jeremiah in his playpen and stretched out on the floor to thumb through a box of albums she'd been planning to donate. There was no more dancing in their house. Any music played had to start with "glory" and end in "hallelujah."

She came across three J. Prince albums, each dedicated "To the one who loved me when I was unlovable."

"I hope you're not about to start playing any music," the Reverend said, already exasperated.

"I wouldn't dream of it," she responded, her sarcasm lost on him.

Watching the Reverend at his desk, disinterested in her presence, Aliyah wondered how she'd allowed herself to end up in this place.

She met Jay on her twenty-first birthday at a downtown club where he and his band were playing. Under the dizzying lights, he spotted her wearing a cheap paper crown her friends forced on her to announce the milestone. She looked cute fidgeting with the spaghetti string tank top she obviously wasn't used to wearing.

"I think we've got a birthday girl in the house y'all!" he

shouted over the roaring crowd. A spotlight was turned on her as the screaming and whistling crowd pushed her toward the stage. She was hoisted up and faced him as he seductively sang "Happy Birthday." He fell at her feet, leaned back as if pleading for her affection, and let out a long, smooth falsetto "youuuuuuu" before the lights faded. She thought she was standing there alone until she felt a hand slip around her waist just as the lights came back up.

"Take your bow," he said before pulling her backstage with him.

"You're crazy," she said, her face flushed with embarrassment.

"No, I'm Jay," he joked. "And you are?"

"Aliyah."

"Well, Princess Aliyah," he said giving a playful nod to the crown on her head and kissing her hand, "I play here every Saturday night. I hope this won't be the last time I see you."

It wasn't. She started coming every Saturday night to watch him perform. Afterward, he'd find her and they'd laugh over rounds of some sinful sounding drink until her friends reminded her she had church in the morning.

"You better get home before the elders come looking for you," he teased. Then one night he invited her out for pancakes at an all-night cafe. That's where he kissed her. Both of them tasted like maple syrup.

Her mother met her at the door at 3:00 a.m. "It's not

proper for a pastor's daughter to be up in a nightclub all hours of the night, bumping and grinding with some R & B singer," she scolded.

But Aliyah wasn't bumping and grinding. She was falling in love.

Other than her father, Jay was the only man who'd asked about her dreams and what she wanted to do with her life. It was decided for her that she would be a teacher, get married, and have a family. Her most righteous mother had pushed several "good, godly" men her way. They didn't care that she'd been the class valedictorian in high school, learned to play the piano solely by listening to the musicians in church, had been voted the best new teacher of the year at her school, or dreamed of writing the great American novel. She was cute, had an hourglass figure, and was the kind of woman men could show off to their friends and still introduce to their mothers. More than one had set his sights on being the first to get her into bed. When their disappointment and impatience grew, they usually politely stopped calling, prompting her mother to ask what she did wrong.

But Jay wanted to know everything about her—her favorite foods, favorite books, what made her laugh, and what made her cry. He made a point of giving her a pink and white star lily after his shows, and he didn't think she was weird for preferring them over roses.

In the four weeks they'd been together, Jay hadn't mentioned sex. Some nights they would lay on the Futon in his sparse studio apartment watching a movie with their legs wrapped around each other. He stroked her hair and she rested her head on his chest. She could feel his heartbeat pounding faster as the warmth of their bodies intensified. He didn't pretend to know the Bible or church rituals, but he respected her. When he told her he loved her, she believed him and she felt safe enough to stay cuddled in his arms until they fell asleep.

"Marry me," he said unexpectedly one night. He'd just finished a show and was still dripping with sweat as he pulled her to him.

Jay reached into a drawer and pulled out a ring with a simple diamond stud in the center. Aliyah guessed the purchase had swallowed up a few of his paychecks.

"I know it's not much, but I promise, one day I'll have you balling in diamonds."

Aliyah's mind raced to find words, but nothing came out of her mouth. Paralyzing panic swept through her body. She couldn't marry Jay. Her mother would feign death and her father would furiously disapprove. Jay was unchurched. Aliyah wasn't even sure he believed in Jesus. But she loved him. She swallowed hard, cupped her hand around his, and nodded yes.

He leaned in to kiss her, and she felt herself collapsing in his arms, not thinking about her parents or the aftermath of what she had done. Jay pressed her back against the wall and her fingers caressed his neck.

"I should get out of these sweaty clothes," he

whispered in her ear. Before he could move, his self-appointed manager burst into the dressing room. When he saw them, he looked away quickly and apologized before going on excitedly about a major record producer being in the audience and wanting to talk to Jay.

"He's only got fifteen minutes before he leaves for the airport. Come on man!"

And that quickly, Jay's ship came in. He was signed on as the opening act for a major U.S. concert tour and had a record deal. He begged Aliyah to join him on the road, but she was afraid. Maybe this was a sign. Her life was in Chestnut Falls as her mother said, and she couldn't make Jay choose between his dream and her.

"You're the first and the last girl I'll ever love," Jay said, resting his palm against her cheek and promising her he'd be back soon before climbing onto the bus that would take him to far more exciting places than Chestnut Falls.

She watched the tour bus fade out of sight, hating herself for not being brave enough to live life and trust love. She hadn't even shown anyone the ring he'd given her, though she took it out of her purse every night and dreamed of the day they'd be together forever.

The tour kicked off in New York and he sent her tickets to the first few shows. It was just a train ride away, and she went despite her mother's objections. The reviews were good. Jay was starting to get more press than the headliner and the record label was ready for his album.

The two days a week he got off (that he'd set aside to see Aliyah) were now spent in L.A., and the J. Prince project was underway. She would call and leave messages. Every day when she came home from work she'd ask her mother if she had any messages or mail. The answer was always the same. After four months of silence, she cried herself to sleep for the last time and finally agreed to go out on a blind date with the Reverend.

Her parents had been badgering her to meet him, convinced they were a perfect match; but, they were as surprised as everyone else when they got engaged just six weeks later.

She should have gotten on that bus and left with Jay, she thought. Her reminiscing and regretting was interrupted when the phone rang. It had to be the church. It was always the church. She begrudgingly answered and was surprised to hear Lena's giddy voice on the other end.

"Good evening, Sister Aliyah," she started, almost hyperventilating with excitement and nerves. "I'm sorry to bother you at home, but I . . . I . . . I've decided to walk in faith and go ahead and plan for lunch with you and Sister Connie next Saturday," she stammered.

Silence.

"I'm an excellent cook if I do say so myself," she said, laughing nervously.

More silence.

"If you can't make it, I'll totally understand, but know that the food will be ready at 1:00 p.m."

She rattled off her address and general directions, followed by, "Have a blessed day," before hanging up.

Aliyah almost genuinely smiled for the first time in a long time.

Chapter 3

Connie peered intently into her dressing room mirror, inspecting herself for new wrinkles. The first ones had been an unwelcome surprise. Now her everyday ritual was covering them up with some of the complimentary products full of questionable promises that she was required to peddle on her show. She ran her nervous hands through a few strands of hair, thinning nearly to non-existence due to years of hot stage lights, chemical treatments, and constant spraying and teasing. She imagined the frozen horrified stares of her audience if she ever dared to walk out on stage without one of her now-famous signature wigs. But it couldn't compare to the shock they'd suffer if they saw her nursing a miniature bottle of alcohol.

The assortment of liquors was hidden discreetly in the drawer of her makeup table. Each had its own special purpose—one to help her sleep, another to erase unpleasant memories. Most were silent friends during dark nights filled with loneliness. Jack Daniels was for show time.

She couldn't remember when stage fright started. Maybe it was when she and the Bishop went national. Maybe when wardrobes, make-up, hair, and ratings took precedence over the gospel and saving souls. She could still hear the cameraman who suggested she consider losing a few pounds. "After all, two million people are watching," he said for motivation. Maybe it was after the letters started coming—letters full of money and pleas for healings, healings they were too proud to admit they couldn't offer.

"Thirty seconds 'til curtain time, Sister Connie," the production manager yelled through the door.

She tipped her head back, tossing down a quick drink, and then dashed a few liquid mint drops on her tongue. Her hands were steadier already.

She rehearsed her smile, put on her wig, and headed for her mark on stage.

"God is good all the time!" she and the Bishop shouted jubilantly over the full band as they emerged from behind the gold lamé curtains.

"And all the time God is good!" the audience roared back, followed by thunderous applause.
The band picked up the pace, and as the show closed, Connie and the Bishop stood center stage

holding hands, smiling, and waving goodbye to the audience. As the lights dimmed and the curtains came down, they slipped their hands free. Connie's assistant was waiting backstage with a bottle of water and some comfortable flats to exchange for her six-inch sequined heels. The Bishop's armor bearer helped him remove his suit jacket and directed him to the editing room. His assistant followed and closed the door behind them.

They taped most shows for at least two hours just to get it down to an hour of power-packed spiritual energy. They would add the opening theme song performed by a citywide choir the Bishop had put together and pick the best crying shots as a teaser to this week's program. Connie and the Bishop used to edit the show together, but he rarely asked for her help anymore now that he had a production team.

"Sister Connie, can I get you something?" her assistant asked as Connie stood at the door to the editing room. She thought about knocking. But why should she knock.

"Bring me my car. I'm going home."

Connie's eyes rolled near the back of her head when she heard Lena's voice on her answering machine. "Jeezus,"

she thought aloud, fast-forwarding the message in mid-sentence. She grabbed a bottle of wine and a glass from her vanity. It was an odd place to keep wine, but it was discreet.

The house was empty, and she'd stopped trying to predict when the Bishop would be home. Piled on her side of the bed were guest lists, scripts, and songs for next week's show. She shoved them aside and fell onto the bed, staring at the larger than life oil painting of the two of them—his monument to himself. Sadly, the painting looked more alive than she felt.

Time had gone by so fast. One day she was a twenty-something, carefree college co-ed, and the next, a middle-aged woman trying to hold on to her youth, sanity, and husband.

They both should have run in the other direction the minute they saw each other. Connie, one of the prettiest and wildest girls on campus and the Bishop, a member of the eclectic "Preacher Boys" who wore suits, carried Bibles, and lead morning prayer every day on the library steps.

"Perhaps you'd do me the pleasure of joining me one evening for dinner," the Bishop said, deliberately interrupting the flirtatious banter between her and a table of school athletes. He didn't flinch as she looked him over in a puff of her cigarette smoke. He carried himself like an old man, but he was good looking and persistent.

And surprisingly, she liked that. But with her reputation, she was reluctant to go out with one of God's chosen. But the bishop was not nearly as innocent as she had imagined all those times she'd declined to go out with him.

On their first date, he slipped his hands under her sweater and his tongue delicately into her mouth. "That's called a French kiss," he boasted, as if a girl like Connie wouldn't already know that. She hid her laughter, not wanting to hurt his feelings.

More dates followed and one night he invited her to spend the night at his apartment.

"God forgive me," he whispered as he took her into his arms and began battling the adversarial desires of his flesh and his soul.

"We have to pray right now," he demanded, pulling her out of the bed and to her knees. A drowsy Connie watched as sweat and tears poured down his flushed face and he literally pleaded with God to cleanse him. It was the first time she'd ever felt like a stain. Each night, the Bishop came to Connie's bed and then regretfully beat his flesh before God. It didn't take long before Connie started feeling compelled to fall to the floor, callout God's name and seek redemption and strength to fight temptation. That strength came too late.

"I'm pregnant," she told him tearfully as he entered her room. His starched dress shirt was already halfway unbuttoned. He didn't say a word as he turned and walked out the door. He looked right through her the few times they passed each other on campus, and it didn't take Connie long to become convinced of what she had to do. Before time ran out she hopped in her car and drove 100 miles to nowhere to handle her problem.

At an out of the way log cabin, discoverable only by those who had a reason to be looking for it, she found a door key discretely placed under an artificial potted plant. Inside, the room was dark and vacant except for a long sofa and a table lamp that sat high on stacked milk crates. She thought about sitting down, but unidentifiable stains on the aged sofa changed her mind. Within minutes a car pulled up. A woman came inside.

"A friend in need?" she asked.

"Is a friend indeed," Connie responded on cue as she had been instructed.

The woman moved quickly, spreading a plastic liner on the sofa and whispering orders for Connie to disrobe and lie down. As the woman tugged and pulled at Connie's flesh, she could feel the heat from the lamp. This stranger prodded and scraped until there was nothing left. Quiet tears rolled down the side of Connie's face. The woman moved from the end of the sofa and handed Connie a brown, unlabeled bottle filled with white pills.

"Take one of these three times a day for a week. You can rest for a half hour then you have to go," she said before turning out the light and leaving.

Connie laid there in the dark, her body shaking and throbbing, her mind cursing the Bishop.

A month later she finally heard from him again.

"We have to get married," he said. No attempts at romance. No bent knee or flowers. Not even a ring. She didn't have the courage to say no or to tell him what she'd done. Besides, who else would have a woman with her reputation and who would probably never be able to give him any legitimate children.

She stood with him at the altar of the campus chapel and said their vows in front of an exuberant young minister whose name they didn't even know. The Bishop promised to get her a ring in a month. She promised to make him proud to have her as his wife.

Connie stared at the two people in the oil painting, barely even recognizing herself. She raised her tired body up, poured herself a drink, and climbed back into bed, wishing she could get the room even darker than it was. She played Lena's message again. Hearing her voice did more than just get on Connie's nerves; it down right angered her. Nobody could be that happy.

Chapter 4

When Lena pulled into her reserved parking space, the church parking lot was alive with cars and people greeting one another and making their way into the building. She smiled proudly at the sign that read, "Reserved for First Lady."

She entered the church and took her place beside her husband, savoring the applause from the standing congregation. It was the one Sunday she would be allowed to join him on the stage. The sanctuary looked even more majestic than the blueprints had suggested.

When she and Pastor Richard took their seats, the choir promptly stood behind them, leading the congregation in a rendition of "Oh Happy Day." The church's full band was packed neatly into the orchestra pit, joyfully playing along as the congregation clapped and moved out into the aisles to dance. Pastor Richard motioned for Lena to rise again and they stood together and sang with the choir, swaying back and forth.

As the choir closed out its final selection, Pastor Richard took his place behind the pulpit and began his message. A large overhead screen descended from the ceiling, projecting each referenced scripture verse. Lena inhaled the admiration of the crowd. All of her life, she had wanted to be somebody special. Today, she was.

"This is the day that the Lord has made!" Pastor Richard shouted to the standing room only crowd.

Lena rushed into Pastor Richard's office, tossed her church hat on the sofa, threw her arms around him, and planted kisses on his neck, cheek, and lips. The deacons struggled to keep their eyes on the stack of money in front of them. A few cleared their throats to remind the young first lady of their presence. Lena ignored them, growing even more affectionate with every cough. A blushing Pastor Richard put his arm around her and gave her a quick peck on the lips, hoping to satisfy her until they got home.

"Well, if that's all I get . . . " she said, feigning irritation. She scooped up her hat with one hand and placed it properly on her head and even pulled out her gloves for effect. "My apologies *Pastor* Richard. I just wanted to tell you what a great job you did out there."

Before she could get her gloves on, he took her hand and kissed her on her palm. His eyes told her there was more where that came from and she gave him a knowing smile.

He peeled off his sweat-soaked robe and tossed it in his chair. He had preached the church into a standing frenzy that drew twenty new converts down the aisle to receive Christ, bringing the official membership up to 2,000. He was emotionally and physically spent and had hoped for a moment of peace and quiet even from Lena. But there was no escaping the trustees and deacons who invaded his office every Sunday after service.

"Yes sir, you preached a powerful message," the head deacon echoed. "But what I don't understand is how we could have over 2,000 people in attendance and barely collect $3,000."

"I'll tell you how. You're preaching to a bunch of God-robbing heathens. That's how," the secretary huffed.

For several minutes they went back and forth about how to fund the $3 million renovations. The trustees suggested he preach messages on tithes and offerings and the deacons insisted they curb spending. Pastor Richard's hand slid away from Lena's. He moved toward his desk and fell into his chair. Massaging his temples and growing weary of the debate raging in his office, he asked in an eerily soft voice, "Who is the pastor?"

Everyone in the room stopped, unsure of whether he had actually spoken.

"Who is the pastor?" he asked again, his voice noticeably louder, punctuating each word.

"You are," a deacon finally answered.

"That's right; I am. I am the anointed one. I am the chosen shepherd to lead the sheep. I am the one who sets the vision for this house."

Everyone was silent, not yet sure whose side of the argument he was on, waiting for him to choose an ally from among the trustees or the deacons.

"From now on, I will handle the money," he announced instead.

They stood gape-mouthed, looking at each other for some clue as to what should be said and who should say it. It didn't take long for one to speak up.

"Now, hold on, Pastor," a senior trustee said, flailing his arms as he made his way toward Pastor Richard. "This church has been here for fifty years. I've been a member for thirty years and a trustee for fifteen years. We've never handed the money over to the pastor, and I don't think we should start now. In fact, I can tell you right now we're not going to do it."

"So, you don't trust your leader?" Pastor asked with the quiet intensity of a predator about to devour its unsuspecting prey. Eyes fell to the floor.

The senior trustee didn't answer immediately, and Lena prayed he was choosing his words carefully.

"You're just a man," he said, throwing fuel onto a smoldering fire.

Pastor Richard circled the room and stood in each person's face, his nose within an inch of theirs, challenging them to look him in the eye.

"Do you trust me?" he asked one deacon. His voice was hard. The deacon gave a timid nod.

"What about you?" he turned to another.

"Yes, Pastor, without a doubt," was the response.

This went on until he'd questioned everyone in the room. They all hurriedly assured him that he had their full trust. How could they not? They had grown to 2,000-strong, had just christened a state-of-the art sanctuary, were distributing meals to the hungry each day, and restoring a community that had been left in ruins. Hope was returning to a part of town life had spit on and forgotten about. To doubt the Pastor seemed like questioning God.

"I guess that means only one person in this room doesn't trust me enough to handle the church's money," he said, turning back toward the elderly trustee. "Maybe it's time for one of us to go. Who should it be? Eenie, meenie, miney, mo. Looks like you're the lucky one out the door."

The trustee turned fire engine red and waited for someone to protest. When no one came to his defense, he launched into a tirade.

"Now, wait just a minute; this demands a vote!" he said angrily.

"A vote? Okay, is there anybody in here who thinks this disloyal Judas should remain on the trustee board?"

No one moved or said a word.

"Looks like it's unanimous," Pastor Richard said as he opened the door and swung his arm to direct the trustee out of his office.

"Thank you for your tireless years of service," he said before slamming the door. "Now, would anyone else like to join him?"

Lena examined their shell-shocked faces. They were either afraid to speak or unsure of what to say, so they all kept quiet.

"Good, then you're all excused. I'll expect all the deposit books and bank records on my desk in the morning. And another thing, this is *my* office. From now on no one comes in without an invitation or appointment."

They filed out of his office, staring past Lena. She didn't know what to make of her husband's self-proclaimed authority or their willingness to accept it.

Pastor Richard fell onto his couch and took a long satisfying drink of water. He stretched out and closed his eyes. Lena sat beside him waiting for him to say something. But he didn't.

"Honey?" she started to question.

He held up his hand to silence her. "Please, sweetheart, not now."

Lena and Richard had been driving around for an hour. She wasn't sure what he was looking for, but things just felt right when they pulled up to the little white wood frame church sitting at the back of a dead end road. Across the street were a group of dilapidated houses— some obviously long abandoned—a pawnshop that was closed on Sundays, and a lonely funeral home with a tired little flower shop connected to it.

About twenty people were inside the church offering the sporadic "Amen" as an elderly man stood in the pulpit delivering the Word. There were no microphones and his voice faded in and out as if he were really only talking to himself.

"The doors of the church are open. Come to Jesus," he finally invited, as a skinny little girl in pigtails who couldn't have been any more than ten years old traded places with him. Her head was barely peeking over the podium, but she began singing "Precious Lord" with the force and conviction of an old soul who had been brought out of the depths of hell by the very hand of God. The sparse crowd was on its feet beckoning to her, "Sing, child!" At that moment, Pastor Richard heard his call to preach. He led Lena to the altar and, over the jubilant claps, announced that God had called him to revive His house. They gathered around him and Lena, laying hands on them and speaking in a garbled unrecognizable language. It didn't matter that he'd never been to seminary or preached one sermon.

"God has answered our prayers," the older man said majestically. "All in agreement?"

"Amen!" they shouted.

Lena felt the soft brush of a flower petal against her cheek. She had closed her eyes tightly when she heard the Pastor tipping into the bedroom, hoping to avoid an unpleasant conversation. She opened her eyes to find him sitting beside her with a large bouquet of red roses. He looked humble, even remorseful. Lena sat up, rubbing pretend sleep from her eyes and ready to talk. He pressed his fingertips to her lips.

"I know I seemed really hard today," he said gently. "But God has started a mighty work and we can't let people get in the way. Remember when Jesus cleaned out the temple? It wasn't nice, but it was necessary. Do you trust me?"

She always did.

"I've just never seen you like that before," she said.

"And, God willing, you never will again."

The roses were beautiful. But she didn't need roses, she needed him and she was quick to welcome him as he climbed under the covers beside her.

Chapter 5

The humidity fell like a wool blanket on the church. A wave of cardboard fans, compliments of the local funeral home, fluttered back and forth along each pew, offering imagined relief. Miss Margaret's screeching rendition of "Amazing Grace" only increased the congregation's discomfort.

With each stream of sweat that raced between the powder-covered folds of her neck, Miss Margaret grew louder and louder, hollering over the piano until the popular hymn was barely recognizable. The congregation held its breath until she released her last out-of-tune note, concluded with a brief holy dance and shout, and reclaimed her seat on the front pew.

"Well, bless the Lord," the Reverend said, clearing his throat and careful not to say anything that would encourage an encore. "Brothers and sisters, if you can't take the heat in here you definitely can't take the fiery furnace of hell."

The church members chuckled and squirmed in their seats, trying to maneuver into the path of the warm breeze coming from the overhead fans. Aliyah glared at him with an "I told you so" smirk. She had warned the Reverend to get the air conditioning checked before summer took hold of his flock. As usual he had ignored her suggestion. She could only hope he'd make his sermon brief. She'd skimmed his notes at the house and knew he'd settled on discussing the submitted wife, again.

"Ladies turn to your husbands and tell them that you are the queen of your house," he said a few weeks ago to an ecstatic group of women who laughed and gave each other high fives.

Just wait, Lena thought dreading the other shoe that was about to drop.

"Now men, turn to your wives and tell her you are the king and you run the kingdom." The men roared while the same women who had just jumped out of their seats in jubilation sat with their arms folded and lips pursed together.

"Don't get mad now sisters, I'm just telling you what saith the Lord," he tried to tease.

He'd gone on to do a four-week series.

"Sisters you take on all these things you don't have to. Let your husband be the leader and trust that he's got you."

Trust that he's got you. Like Aliyah trusted him to pick up some diapers for Jeremiah on his way home one day. He forgot and she had to struggle out in a thunderstorm because despite her pleas he refused to believe that they couldn't make it through the night with just four diapers. "If you insist on going out, can you grab me some snacks for the office?" he called out as she slammed the door. Or like she trusted him to take turns feeding Jeremiah so that she could get just a few more hours of sleep some nights.

"This is ridiculous," he said after making his one and only midnight trip to the nursery. "I have to get up and go to the church office in the morning. You'll be home and can sleep all day."

His final message in the series was titled, "A Nagging Wife Isn't a Submitted Wife." He shot a few quick glances her way when he preached that message.

She couldn't imagine how he had anything else to say, but she knew it was an endless topic for him. There was certainly nothing else that she cared to hear on the subject. Fortunately, the baby needed a diaper change—her weekly excuse to exit the sanctuary and return at her pleasure.

Just as she got up from her seat and prepared to politely slip out, he unexpectedly called for "his beautiful first lady" to join him in the pulpit. A member of the Mother's Board gently took Jeremiah out of her arms and a deacon escorted her to the Reverend's side.

He had an important announcement to make, he told the anxiously waiting congregation.

After months of backroom evaluations and debates, the Reverend was officially a candidate for presiding bishop of the International Pentecostal Church Council. The call came in minutes before the start of morning service. As the pastor of a beloved historic church and the son-in-law of an even more loved former presiding bishop, he was the candidate to beat and he was assured he was a shoo-in if he did as he was told. There was no discussion, no asking Aliyah for her opinion, just an exuberant "I accept!" from the Reverend. The church exploded into celebration and Aliyah stood beside him trying to muster a smile.

Aliyah was solemn and quiet on the ride home from church. She couldn't have gotten a word in edge wise anyway because one of the church Elders had invited himself to their house and took the front seat, leaving Aliyah in the back with Jeremiah. He and the Reverend talked excitedly during the whole drive. The phone started ringing the moment they got home. Aliyah went to put Jeremiah down in his crib and pulled the Reverend aside.

"We need to talk," she tried to whisper. He'd made a huge decision and she wasn't sure he really knew what was in store for their family. She was also afraid to think about what it meant for her. As a child, Aliyah had watched with intrigue and even pride when her own father was nominated for the prestigious post. His win made her family church royalty in the national and international Protestant community. He made three national appearances each year. At each one, thousands would stand to their feet upon the arrival of the presiding bishop and the first family. Her father led the way into the convention hall, his robe flowing and Bible tucked visibly under his arm. The position of presiding bishop was special, although Aliyah never understood what it had to do with godliness. She still didn't. But, she knew the extra stress and strain it had put on her mother to be perfect.

"Reverend I can grab that phone for you if you want," the Elder called out from the living room. He was already trying to position himself as an invaluable member of the Reverend's team.

"Yes, please grab it. I'll be right there," he said "Aliyah, I don't have time for this right now."

"Maybe you out to make the time," she said.

"Look, can you just be happy for one day? Just one day; that's all I'm asking."

He walked out of the nursery and took call after call until well after midnight.

It was 2:00 a.m. before Aliyah finally managed to get Jeremiah settled into sleep. The shrill ringing of the phone woke him again at 5:00 a.m. The Reverend paced around the bedroom cradling the phone between his ear and shoulder while trying to write. "God's will be done," he said repeatedly, thanking callers for their support and pledged donations.

Aliyah pulled the comforter over her head and sank deeper into the bed trying to ignore Jeremiah's cries and block the rays of sunlight that were peeking through the curtains. She'd had maybe three hours of sleep if you counted the thirty minutes she'd spent in the wooden rocking chair with a pillow propped under her head. The Reverend couldn't sleep with Jeremiah in their bed, so she often drifted off while rocking him only to have her sleep disrupted to move to their bed later.

"Aliyah, Jeremiah is crying," the Reverend said just above a whisper as he covered up part of the phone. When she didn't respond he nudged her.

"I need you to get this. I'm on the phone."

With one hand, she threw the covers back and glared at him as he walked out of the room, strategizing his first church campaign event.

Chapter 6

Connie and the Bishop sat regally in their gold high-back chairs. They wore matching white suits that they would never have worn on television. The stark white would bleach out their skin on camera. But the Bishop had decided a long time ago that no matter how successful they became, Sunday service was not to be televised. It was a holy day.

The congregation, most of them tourists who'd stood in line for hours waiting for one of the limited Sunday morning seats, piled in. Many carried cameras that were quickly confiscated by the church's security staff. Praise dancers glided across the stage, mimes performed in the aisles, and ushers scurried about trying to get everyone in place before the Bishop moved to the podium to take control over his circus.

"Good morning, brothers and sisters," his gentle

voice amplified throughout the auditorium. "We are so glad you're here!"

On cue, the keyboardist and drummer played in unison, moving everyone to their feet. After a sufficient number of people were up dancing and clapping, the Bishop threw up his fist and the music instantly stopped.

"Hallelujah," he proclaimed over the cries of the audience. "Take your seats if the spirit will let you while my lovely wife opens us in prayer."

The Bishop held out his hand to her. She walked past him without taking it and stared at the eager faces waiting for nothing more than to hear her voice. "Start softly and calmly, then move into a more pleading cry, finally raising your voice to a victorious shout," he had trained her years ago.

Connie wished he'd taken the pastoral internship he was offered. But he was too burdened by the shame of being unable to explain how Connie was three months pregnant when they'd only been married for a few weeks. Despite his efforts to purify their union—he imposed a month of celibacy to rid them of the Jezebel spirit and they held hands and jumped into the lake to baptize each other— he waited painfully for the punishment he believed God was going to inflict. When Connie "miscarried" he was certain that was God's merciful way of giving them a second chance to get right with Him.

Connie looked over the checkbook and punched

numbers into the calculator. She did the math twice and finally resolved herself to the fact that she and the Bishop had $250 to their names after paying the rent on their meager one-bedroom apartment. She could only hope that one of her auditions for a local theater production might pan out. Now that there was no more baby, the Bishop agreed to let her try to find a job. But all she'd planned for was being an actress.

Looking at their depleted funds, she felt foolish agreeing to spending any money for three weeks of community television access time.

"God is speaking to me," the Bishop insisted. "He's got a big assignment for us and this is the first step."

Connie thought maybe he'd had a slight breakdown— her fault for corrupting his light with her darkness. She didn't say anything when he started preaching on the courthouse steps, especially if that's what it took to bring him back to sanity. She would stand off in the distance watching as he went every day at lunchtime, dressed in the same suit, Bible in hand, and preached a message of salvation and repentance to anyone who would stop and listen. Surprisingly, people did stop. Initially it was out of curiosity, but there was something about his compassion and warm charm that often drew them in. He made them feel as if he really cared about their souls, and Connie was sure that he did. Often, before he left, there would be at least ten people gathered around him for prayer and giving him a few dollars to use as "seed" for his ministry.

He'd gotten the nickname "Boardwalk Bishop" from the regular lunch goers. But Connie was convinced God's plan was to go from the sidewalk to a television studio.

One lone camera faced two chairs with a small wooden table between them. The Bishop could choose between a sky blue or black background and place whatever props he wanted on the table. Most people went with a coffee cup or plant, but the Bishop chose a huge Bible and propped it up on a picture stand. A cameraman appeared from behind a barely visible door in the back of the studio.

"When you see the red light start talking," he dryly instructed. "I'll be back in twenty minutes to shut everything down."

The studio lights were blinding, and being confined to a chair made him more nervous and restless. He was used to the openness of the outdoors and personal interaction with people. He stammered his way through some notes, shared the Biblical roadmap to salvation, and offered prayer to anyone who might be watching.

"Did you see the show? How was it?" he asked Connie when he got home. She could be gentle and diplomatic or brutally honest.

"It needs some work," she finally said hesitantly.

He knew she was telling the truth, but he was still disappointed.

"But you've got two more shows and I can help you," she reassured. "If this is for God, let's make it the best it can be—together."

His face lit up in a way that it hadn't since they'd been married.

"Yes . . . together!" he said, offering her a genuine hug.

The Bishop balked at having to wear makeup.

"Under these cheap lights, you'll look like a ghost without it," Connie warned.

She got rid of the chairs and table and grouped together a few artificial plants that were stuck in a supply closet. She coached him on speaking from his diaphragm, standing up straight so he would look even taller, and treating the camera like a person.

"Pretend you are on those courthouse steps," she said right before the cameraman pushed record. Connie sat in a chair beneath the lens so he could look at her while he was talking. He didn't take his eyes off of her even as he enjoyed the freedom of walking the floor and preaching. He took direction well and looked natural as he pleaded with the lost and distraught to bring their burdens to God.

"You may be sick. You may be tired. You may be broke, busted, and disgusted. But you are not alone brothers and sisters!" he fired off without taking a breath. "God is with you and with God on your team, you will never lose no matter what the scoreboard looks like!"

And without thinking, he gave out his phone number and encouraged anyone to call for prayer.

That night, the Bishop got three callers. One man was

contemplating suicide. He made a deal with God that he'd hold on one more night if someone picked up the phone. The Bishop spent an hour talking to him. Another caller had a sick child. She said God told her calling the Bishop was the first step in building her faith. He told her to place the child near the phone and began to pray for healing and restoration. More people called as the week went on. Many wanted to know how to donate to his ministry. He didn't' have an answer for that. He hadn't even thought about the money, but Connie saw a new life in him—a new joy that excited her.

"What do you think about joining me on camera for this last show?" he asked Connie right before the taping. "You could close the show with a song."

Connie was surprised that the Bishop remembered she could sing. He'd only heard her a couple of times.

"Okay," she said reluctantly. "What do you want me to sing?"

"Just let God use you," he said before the camera started rolling.

The Bishop spent most of the twenty-minute show sharing prayer requests he'd received and thanking viewers for letting this "humble servant of God" into their lives.

"We've only had a short time together, but I hope it's been a good time. And I can't end this show without introducing you to my better half. My prime rib," he joked.

Connie joined him on the small set and gripped the

microphone she'd been given. There was no time for a mic check. She wasn't afraid of the camera or singing, but unlike the Bishop, she had not spent her life in church. She strained to think of anything other than a Christmas carol until she had a sudden flashback of her grandmother singing and praising God around the house. She pulled "The Old Rugged Cross" from the back of her memory and felt a strange stirring of emotion with each verse. Maybe it was the sweet memory of her grandmother who took care of her when her mother was unwilling or unable. Maybe it was the fact that she was sharing a real moment with the Bishop. Or maybe she had finally let God in.

When she was finished, the cameraman, who usually disappeared as quickly as he appeared, was standing beside the camera watching her and wiping his eyes.

"My name is Derrick," he said. "I've never done this before, but I want to give you this."

He handed the Bishop an envelope with a $300 check inside, enough to keep them on the air for another three shows with a little left over.

The stage lights blinded Connie from the waiting stares of anyone past the third row. "Let us pray," she began, reciting every word that had been scripted for her by the Bishop now rolling across the teleprompter Derrick was operating.

Chapter 7

The lunch date had finally come. It had been an unseasonably dry spring and the burst of rain was an unexpected surprise. Lena watched Aliyah sprint from her car, clutching her umbrella and fighting the wind through the hard raindrops pelting against her kitchen window. Lena had spent days reading over and memorizing her mentors' profiles in the FLS membership book. Aliyah came from three generations of preachers. Her great-grandfather founded one of the city's oldest and largest churches. Her grandfather followed him as pastor for forty years. Aliyah's father stepped into his shoes later, baptizing the children of some of the city's most influential people. Aliyah graduated with honors with a degree in early childhood education and taught first grade before marrying an up-and-coming pastor in the church her family built. They've been married for three years and have a five-month-old son named Jeremiah.

There was no sign of Connie, the art lover and former theater major. Her bio didn't mention any children, just the multi-million dollar studio she and her husband founded fifteen years ago with little more than $1,000 and a hand-held camera. Now their program was syndicated in every major market in the United States and they were set to go international in just a few months.

"Come in! Come in!" Lena squealed, pulling Aliyah inside.

"Whew, it's a mess out there," she said, shaking the rain off like a wet dog. "I didn't think I was going to make it."

"I'm glad you did," Lena said. Aliyah followed Lena into the kitchen and Lena poured her a cup of hot tea.

"We can eat now or wait for Sister Connie," Lena said, hoping she'd choose to eat.

"I'm okay. We can wait."

Lena wasn't quite sure what to do with her even though she seemed content sipping her tea. Her eyes followed a collection of magnets that covered Lena's refrigerator—everything from clowns, angels, fruits, and insects to a reindeer made out of Popsicle sticks. Realizing Aliyah was looking at them, Lena felt a little embarrassed by the gaudy display.

"They're from when I was a little girl. My grandmother and I used to make them," she spoke up.

"I keep them to remind me of her." She had only been dead for a year and Lena missed her terribly.

"That's sweet," Aliyah said. "Hold on to things that matter to you."

Aliyah could tell Lena's kitchen was used a lot. Cookbooks were stacked along the counter, fresh produce decorated the table, and a small patch of herbs grew in her windowsill. But any chance of more conversation was cut short by the frantic irritated ringing of the doorbell. Connie had arrived.

"Well, it took you long enough!" Connie exploded as she dashed inside and patted her wig to make sure it was securely in place. She handed Lena her dripping umbrella as if she were the hired help without even so much as a grunt hello. Her face softened slightly when she noted the freshly pressed linen tablecloth on the dining room table. It set Lena and Pastor Richard back $50. The flatware, although not real silver, was shining and appropriately arranged, as were the other dishes. Lena had studied. Connie was pleased. Today might not be a complete waste of time.

The ladies ate in relative quiet, and then Lena dutifully brought out dessert and coffee.

"Well that was a nice little lunch," Connie commented, although it didn't really sound like a compliment coming from her.

"It's obvious you can cook, but being a member of FLS is about more; you know?"

Here it comes, thought Aliyah, *another lecture on*

the historical value and standard of excellence that FLS represents. She'd gotten that speech when she joined. Of course, hers came from her mother.

"How many chapters do we have?" Connie quizzed.

"Twenty throughout the state," Lena answered easily.

"Our oldest and most prestigious committees?"

"Hospitality, scholarship, and helping hands."

"Our purpose?"

"To be a supreme and tireless help mate for our husbands in their mission to feed the hungry, clothe the naked, house the homeless, and save the lost."

Connie reviewed her notes, looked Lena over, and said, "You might have what it takes."

Lena almost dared to smile.

"I said *might,*" Connie quickly repeated.

Connie pulled out several worn notebooks and spread them on Lena's table, crushing the rose petals she'd put down for decoration.

"I told you to become these and I intend to make sure you do."

"Sister Connie's students have won the outstanding new member award for the last four years," Aliyah explained. She didn't tell Lena that all of them stopped speaking to Connie after they got their membership pins.

"And I plan to make it five. This little meal was nice, but you obviously have a lot to learn," she said handing her a book simply titled *Entertaining*. "I'm sure you'll do even better next Saturday."

Aliyah wasn't planning on another Saturday. She had only come to be polite and she certainly wasn't interested in putting what little time and energy she had left into training another FLS member, especially not now with her husband's election. "Maybe we shouldn't impose," she said diplomatically.

Connie cut her eyes at Aliyah. "Is that what we're doing? Are we imposing on you in our effort to help get you into FLS?"

She and Aliyah exchanged cursing glares.

"No, no, not at all," Lena spoke up, nervously. "It would be a pleasure."

"Maybe it will be and maybe it won't be. That depends on how well you study."

With nothing more to say, Connie gathered her things and motioned for Aliyah to follow her. When they got outside, Aliyah could feel the pressure rising in her head. Connie walked with her to the car and gripped Aliyah's door before she could close it.

"I heard the news about your husband. You know an endorsement from me and my husband could seal the deal rather quickly for him. You should think about that," Connie said sharply.

"I'm sure I should," Aliyah shot back as she yanked the door closed, almost catching Connie's hand.

"That girl's got a lot to learn," Connie said smugly under her breath.

Lena sighed with relief, believing the lunch was a success. She wasn't sure whether she *liked* Connie or not, but she could overcome her. She'd been overcoming people like her all of her life. She looked at the pile of dirty dishes on the counter. It would have been nice if they'd stayed around to help clean up. Next time she would use paper plates, if the FLS book said they were proper. She was gathering up the dishes to submerge them in a sink of sudsy water when the telephone rang. She was beginning to hate hearing it ring and was thankful for the answering machine. Right after the beep she heard her mother's voice.

"Lena, baby, it's Mama. I wanted to let you know your daddy is dying. Call me."

A cup slid from her hand and sank to the bottom of the sink as she raced to the phone. "Hello," she said catching the phone just before her mother hung up.

Her *daddy* was dying. Lena mulled over her mother's words. She knew her *daddy* only as Stan and could count on one hand the times she'd talked to him. All she really knew about him was that he and her mother fell in love and ran off to Chicago together. He left them before she was born and came home to make his fortune in the liquor industry, which turned into a car dealership that led to a number of gas stations. He sent for the two of them when Lena was two years old. They wouldn't be his family, just his responsibility. Her first memory of him was when she was about four years old. For a while, on Sundays she would quietly watch him from the backseat of his Cadillac while he and her mother sat talking in the still and secretive darkness of the night. They spoke so softly that Lena couldn't tell what they were saying, but she knew it was time to go when her mother pressed her full fire engine red lips against his and put the large white envelope he always handed her in her purse. Lena's prize for being a good girl was a giant rainbow-colored lollipop. When he passed it to her, she noticed that they had the same green eyes. One morning Aliyah caught her mother sitting at the kitchen table crying over something she'd seen in the weekend newspaper. After that the Sunday visits stopped.

She was six the next time she saw him. He came over late at night when Lena was supposed to be sleeping. "I'm married now. I have more commitments, but I promise I'll get by as much as I can," she heard him say through the walls.

Their last meeting was over ten years ago before Aliyah and her mother packed up their things and moved to the country with her grandparents.

Her mother hummed "Happy Birthday" to herself while putting on make-up by the bare light bulb in the bathroom. It was her thirtieth birthday. Candles filled the house Stan had rented for them, and the sweet smell of perfume traveled effortlessly to each room. He opened the door with his key, carrying roses—her mother's favorite.

"Is that you Stan?" her mother called from her bedroom.

He didn't answer but headed toward her voice, stepping casually over Lena as she lay sprawled out on the floor watching TV.

"It's my birthday. You promised!" her mother cried almost immediately.

"I know, but I can't. Not tonight," he said while walking briskly out of the room. Lena's mother was close at his heels.

"If you go, there's no point in ever coming back." There was a pleading resolve in her voice. "I won't go on like this. We're done."

Stan stood at the door, his hand on the knob, thinking, waiting for something. Then without even saying goodbye, he walked out.

"Did you hear me?" her mother asked.

"Yes I—I heard you," Lena answered slowly, unsure of what she was supposed to say.

"The doctors say he's got a few months. Maybe. They've moved him to hospice. He wants to see you." Her mother's voice was tired and mournful. "Maybe you could come some evening around nine. Visiting hours are over at seven, but they'll let you in."

Lena was sure they would. She and her mother had been hiding all of her life. Deferring to Stan's need to keep them a secret although her mother insisted it was about decency. As if sneaking around in the midnight shadows was decent.

Lena took a deep breath, guarding her words before saying something she'd have to apologize for. "I'll have to think about it," she said.

There was a pause.

"Well, if that's how you feel."

"That's how I feel."

A shivering early morning breeze ran down Lena's bare back. She hated it when the Pastor left the window open overnight. She rolled over to chastise him only to find a single rose beside her with a note: *"Love ya!"* There was no running shower or breakfast aroma rising from downstairs, not that he would ever think to make her breakfast. He was gone and she probably wouldn't see him for the rest of the day. She wondered how many times her mother had woken up to an abandoned bed. Daylight had barely broken through the clouds and she was tempted to go back to sleep. But there was cooking to do—for Aliyah and Connie.

The past three weeks had been mind-numbingly the same. She cooked; they ate; Connie quizzed and criticized; Aliyah offered sympathetic reassurance. Very little conversation flowed between them, but Lena usually didn't mind. A lot could be learned from quiet observation. Most of all, she was happy just to have the company. As much as she hated to admit it, she was growing lonely. She'd never made many friends, relying instead on the Pastor to be her best friend, her confidant, her lover, her everything. But now he spent most of his days at church. Sometimes he didn't come home until bedtime, leaving Lena to eat dinner alone in front of the television. When he did come home, the phone calls started. Whenever she answered, there would be no one on the other end. But when Pastor picked up, he launched into a long intense conversation that often began as a whisper before escalating. She'd asked him what was wrong and he'd always gently tell her there was nothing to worry about, kiss her goodnight, and dart out the door again.

Chapter 8

Another rainy Saturday. The ladies sat silently in the dining room, eating and watching the endless dismal rainfall.

"You really like to cook, don't you," Aliyah finally said, breaking the silence.

"It's a hobby," Lena said proudly. "Do you have any hobbies?"

"Yes, changing diapers," she said unenthused. Lena's girlish giggle made Aliyah smile. "Actually, I used to write."

It seemed strange even mentioning. She hadn't picked up a pen and paper in so long. She had a notebook full of short stories that the Reverend wasn't interested in reading. He'd feigned interest while they were engaged; but once they were married he told her, "Reading made up stories is a waste of time. I'd rather develop my mind with writings from the great religious thinkers."

Jay had loved her stories and poems. They used to talk about all the great songs they were going to write together. Now the only things she wrote out were grocery and to-do lists.

"Used to? Why'd you stop?" Lena asked.

Aliyah didn't' really have an answer. It was just one of many things she no longer had control over.

"If I win, we'll be traveling a lot. It's not like when your Dad was the presiding bishop. I'll have more responsibilities. It won't just be pomp and circumstance," the Reverend had told her, oblivious to the fact that he'd insulted her father's legacy. "It'll be important for you to be right there with me. We'll probably have to get a nanny for Jeremiah."

Aliyah hadn't planned to give up her entire life when she married the Reverend. Then again there were a lot of things she hadn't planned on when *she* proposed to him.

They sat in the corner booth waiting for the waitress to bring dessert. Aliyah found the Reverend polite and not bad looking if you were into the khaki pants, buttoned-down shirt-wearing kind of man. For the last few weeks they'd come to the same restaurant after Bible study and ordered dessert. He always had apple pie and teased Aliyah for always wanting to try something new. They had never kissed, but he'd taken her hand a few times while he walked her to her car or to the door of her parents' home. Seeing them together made her parents happy, especially her mother.

"You are an extraordinary Christian woman," he told her one night.

"Thank you," she said, blushing and shifting her eyes to the television set that was mounted overhead. It was turned to one of those entertainment shows. The sound was muted and Aliyah was surprised when Jay appeared on the screen with his arm wrapped around a beautiful woman.

"I've really enjoyed this time we've spent together," the Reverend went on, even though Aliyah was no longer listening. She was focusing on the words sliding across the bottom of the television screen.

NEW MUSIC SENSATION AND SUPERMODEL RUMORED TO BE EXPECTING THEIR FIRST CHILD.

Aliyah was momentarily frozen, then she felt a bubbling of hurt and anger rising in her chest.

"What I guess I'm trying to say is . . ."

"Marry me," Aliyah interrupted. Her voice was commanding and she leaned in to kiss the Reverend, hoping to erase the taste of Jay's lips from her memory.

"Marry me," she said again.

"Why'd I stop writing? I guess I haven't really had anything to write about," she told Lena.

"What about you, Sister Connie?" Lena asked. "Any hobbies?"

Connie was on her second helping of gumbo and uninterested in engaging in frivolous chatter. Lena sitting and staring at her with a wide-eyed grin only irked her more.

After pausing just long enough to try to make Lena feel ridiculous for having asked the question, Connie confessed, "No, I can't say that I do have a hobby. I spend seven days a week in the studio ministering to millions of people around the world."

"Come on, even you must have had a life before *this*," Lena pressed.

It was hard to remember what life had been like before she and the Bishop set off on their ministry. Before he rescued her, as he liked to say. There was no denying she'd been a sinner—the worst sort—but there had been more to her.

"I used to act," she finally said matter-of-factly as she put down her empty bowl. She actually had hoped to be a Broadway star, but admitting that somehow made her feel like a failure and old.

"This is the only day for another six months you'll be able to get the procedure done," Connie's sorority sister warned.

Connie had spent part of her spring semester book money on a bus ticket to New York and stood in line for hours hoping to get just one of the thirty open audition spots for an upcoming Broadway musical. She was one of only five called back for a final audition for a major supporting role. There might never be another opportunity like this.

"People are getting busted all over the country. You're lucky we found her. I can't guarantee you another chance any time soon to get your situation taken care of."

Connie crumpled up the audition letter and threw it in the trash.

She couldn't remember the name of the woman who got the part, but she walked away with a Tony award that year.

"An actress and a writer, now that's exciting," Lena said. "I could never do anything like that." Her ambitions had been simple: be a good wife, first lady, and, someday, a mother.

"So listen, Lena, we've had seafood the last two Saturdays. I was thinking you could do something with a little ethnic flare next week," Connie said, purposely changing the subject. "Your church is striving to be multicultural, isn't it?"

"Yes, of course," she said, although she'd never really thought about it.

"Some of the most interesting food I've ever eaten was when the Bishop and I went on a missionary trip to Thailand. An oriental menu . . . that would be good," she said, reflecting on the sights and smells of that part of the island where all the tourists landed.

"I've never been outside of the country or even the state," Lena admitted. "It must be so exciting to visit so many different places."

Lena was so refreshingly simple.

Connie thought better of telling her about the malaria, diarrhea, and heat-induced delirium they'd suffered in some of the most ungodly places in the world. Of course that was a long time ago. Now they were usually official guests of some dignitary.

"We've been to some beautiful places. You'd like Kenya. The wildlife is breathtaking. I stood just a few feet from a zebra once."

"Wow. Do you have any pictures?" Lena asked.

Looking through old photos of her and the Bishop rarely ended in her having a good night and she slightly resented Lena for forcing thoughts of the past to run through her mind. Then again, she was the one who'd brought up Thailand.

"Oh, I don't know where they would be. We have so many stored away. If I have time to search, maybe I'll bring some next week."

Chapter 9

The campaign for presiding bishop was in full swing. There were three candidates and they had six weeks to win over convention members. Aliyah's house was being transformed into a church campaign headquarters with an assembly line of church volunteers scattered in the living room stuffing envelopes with bios and pictures. The Reverend had raised $100,000 in the first week of his campaign—more than either of his opponents, although the word opponent was frowned upon. They were fellow brothers in Christ, the Reverend always reminded his team. It didn't take long for Connie and the Bishop to jump on board because, despite Aliyah's behavior, they had every intention of being on the side of a winner. They brought their camera crew to the church on Sunday morning to capture every handshake and hug. Today, they had descended on Aliyah's home with a photographer and stylist to prepare for an exclusive interview and look at the daily life of "God's young servants." The Bishop draped his arms around them, pulling them into an inescapable bear hug. Connie offered a more subdued gesture complete with air kisses on each side of Aliyah's cheeks.

"It's good to see you again, Sister Connie," Aliyah said, trying to mask the air of pretense that existed between them.

Without a television or radio program, the pulpit was the Reverend's only live platform to get his name and agenda before the one-hundred-plus member churches that would be under his leadership. He'd already broken his rule against preaching at other churches on Sunday. He'd once told Aliyah he thought it was a disgrace for pastors to leave the flock God gave them in order to go fleece another. But, he didn't protest when his "spiritual advisors" scheduled a two-week long, fifteen-church speaking engagement stretching across the country. And now he had an open invitation to one of the country's premier Christian broadcast stations.

"I guess you'll have to start showing me a little more respect," Connie mumbled through her camera-ready, fixed smile as their husbands embraced each other.

"One might think," Aliyah quipped.

Had it not been for the family name she bore, Aliyah wouldn't have cared about the election at all.

The stylist fiddled around, talking over ideas with

himself as he studied Aliyah and the Reverend, not that there was much to the Reverend's wardrobe. He would wear his minister's collar and a black jacket. It was important for him to look serious and traditional. There was talk of putting Jeremiah in a suit, but the idea was scrapped after he spit up on his onesie. Even thinking he would sit through a rigid photo shoot was overly ambitious. The real debate was whether Aliyah should wear a hat or not. The photographer said it made her look fake. The stylist, who made it known to everyone that he typically worked with more well known Christian leaders, insisted a hat made her look sophisticated and traditional, which would appeal to older women. Neither asked Aliyah for her opinion. Bickering like an old married couple, they finally decided half the photographs would be with the hat and the other half without. *They* would make a decision later about which one to use. Aliyah graciously ignored them, and just enjoying being pampered. Getting her hair and nails done was a luxury she hadn't indulged in for months. Even the Reverend noticed.

"I like your hair," he said as the photographer posed them, catching Aliyah off guard.

"That young man is really something," the Bishop said as he watched them. Connie knew his mind was working overtime trying to decide what his victory could do for them. They'd spent half the day overseeing things and giving the Reverend advice about his platform even though it was becoming obvious he didn't' really need any help.

"He reminds me of me when I was that age. Full of fire for the Lord."

Connie pretended not to hear him.

Only certain types of FLS members got away with sitting in the back of their husbands' churches unnoticed: new moms and seniors. The thinking was that it was too distracting to have the pastor's wife coming in and out of the sanctuary to tend to the needs of an infant, and senior first ladies didn't need to sit up front. Their position in the church was already well established. For Aliyah, it was being made clear that she would have to become more visible in the church soon. Jeremiah was growing, and once the Reverend became the presiding bishop, her "back of the church" pass would come to an end. It was time for her to take her figurative seat beside the Reverend.

She'd stopped teaching after the Reverend was installed as pastor. She hadn't been that eager to go back to work anyway. Still grieving over her father's death and trying to take care of Jeremiah had taken an unexpected toll on her. But she hadn't planned on her entire life being absorbed into an abyss of responsibilities, expectations, and commitments. There was already talk of assigning her a "helper" as days and nights were running together, distinguishable only by

Jeremiah's morning wailing and her late night collapse into bed.

Most days began at 6 a.m., but the Reverend, suddenly unable to coordinate his own wardrobe, woke her up at 4:30 today to help him pack for his church campaign trip. Any other time she might have been flattered to be needed by him, but she'd been up most of the night with Jeremiah who was teething miserably. He'd only fallen asleep a couple of hours before she felt the Reverend poking her arm and forcing her to critique each shirt and tie combination he pulled from the closet.

"I'll call you when I get to my hotel," is all she remembered him saying as she stumbled back to bed trying to get in at least thirty more minutes of sleep before Jeremiah woke up. She didn't expect it to be 8:00 a.m. when she opened her eyes again, nor did she expect to look out of her window and find Connie standing at her door. She checked Jeremiah, her new mother anxiety eased when she felt his back rise and fall with each soft breath. The nasal buzzing of the doorbell made him squirm, but he stopped short of waking. Aliyah thought about ignoring Connie and crawling back into bed, but she guessed Connie would only keep standing there obnoxiously ringing the bell until someone answered.

"I know it's early and I apologize for not calling," Connie said as soon as Aliyah opened the door. She didn't ask to come inside and Aliyah didn't invite her. "I think we should call a truce."

Connie was dressed for the studio and in full makeup. She looked overdone under the natural light of the morning.

"I didn't know we were at war," Aliyah said dryly, over a slow yawn.

Connie's usually scrunched face softened and she removed the sunglasses that were hiding her blood shot eyes.

"I know I'm not the easiest person to deal with, but we're supposed to be role models for Lena. She has six weeks before she becomes an FLS member and I'd like for us to at least try and show her what that sisterhood represents," Connie said.

The last thing FLS was about was sisterhood—elitism, prestige, and vanity, maybe, but not sisterhood. Connie knew as much. This proposed truce had to have some other purpose, but Aliyah didn't know what. She skeptically shook Connie's hand, sealing their unwritten agreement.

"Very good," Connie said, sounding almost sincere. "I guess I'll see you Saturday."

Aliyah closed the door and waited to wake from her dream.

Connie watched herself on the monitor during playbacks of the promotional spots she and the Bishop had spent the morning taping. There she was in her teased wig and inch-thick makeup nodding and grinning through each line of the Bishop's script. This year he was promising pentecostal power, the unleashing of Holy Ghost power to heal and cast out the demons in people's lives.

"The Spirit of God has spoken to me brothers and sisters. He's ready to move among you and release you from cancer, heart disease, crippling arthritis, and generational poverty. He's just waiting for you to call on Him," the Bishop announced. With Connie standing by his side, he looked passionately into the camera and pleaded with viewers to send their prayer requests for pentecostal power along with a generous seed offering of faith . . . specifically, $50 or more. If history repeated itself, they could expect to bring in some $3 million by the end of the year, though they wouldn't keep any records of how many people actually received a breakthrough.

"So what do you think the Holy Ghost is going to do with all that money?" Connie asked the Bishop, walking off the set before he could answer.

Oriental food wasn't Lena's specialty. All week she'd practiced fried rice, dumplings, hot and sour soup, and egg roll recipes. Nothing tasted as it should. The rice was a goopy paste, the soup too watery, and the dumplings a doughy mess. She could have fed half of China with all the food she'd thrown away. The only things she mastered were the egg rolls—her own crispy blend of water chestnuts, garlic, cabbage, and carrots—but she could make anything taste good with oil and a deep fryer. Beyond that the meal needed serious prayer.

"Your sorority girls coming over again?" Pastor asked, searching the kitchen for signs of something to eat. Not that he was hungry or had time to eat, but this was the third Saturday in a row she hadn't cooked breakfast for him.

"Sisters Connie and Aliyah, yes, and it's not a sorority honey. I wish you'd stop calling it that," Lena answered, not looking up from the napkin she was struggling to fold into a flower.

Inside the refrigerator, Pastor found platters of egg rolls waiting to be dipped into the fryer, bowls of rice, diced vegetables, and spare ribs.

"I'm glad somebody is getting fed around here," he said. He shut the refrigerator door with just enough force to get Lena's attention. She sprang from the table and nervously pulled out a skillet.

"Do you want some eggs? I can make you something."

"Forget about it," he mumbled as he walked out of the kitchen.

Chapter 10

Gospel music makes the garden grow. That was Aliyah's mother's motto. So it wasn't a surprise to hear Mahalia Jackson's powerful voice coming from the backyard or to find her mother hunched over her garden swinging her hips and singing "How I Got Over" to her roses and lilies. This was her idea of cutting loose.

Aliyah eased behind her and turned off the music, careful not to wake Jeremiah who was sleeping on her shoulder.

"Goodness gracious, you scared the daylights out of me," her mother said, whirling around and clutching her chest. She caught her breath and started to laugh.

"Sorry," Aliyah said. She sat on a lawn chair and positioned herself so the beaming sun would not blind her or burn the baby's delicate skin.

"I didn't know you were coming by today," she said,

reaching for Jeremiah while simultaneously pulling off her earth-stained gloves.

"I was hoping you could watch Jeremiah for a couple of hours. I'm having lunch with Sister Connie."

"Of course I'll watch my little angel," she said, reminded of her daughter's impending notoriety. "I had lunch plans, but nothing that can't be changed. So how is the campaign going?"

"Okay, I think. This week alone he's gotten three endorsements."

"Anything from the retiring Bishop?"

"No, he's very sick. We're not even sure he's going to make it to the election."

"I do need to send his family a card. He and your father were wonderful colleagues," her mother said, making a mental note. There was no doubt in Aliyah's mind that her card would also be a gentle reminder to the Bishop's staff to send a formal letter of endorsement for her son-in-law. At this point, the campaign wasn't for actual votes. The Reverend had those. It was for credibility. The presiding bishop post was a four-year position. Confidence in his leadership guaranteed lifelong reelection and the continuation of a six-figure salary. Only twice in the history of the Pentecostal Church Council had there been an involuntary or premature departure. This campaign wasn't about winning; it was about staying.

"I'll be back around 1:00. Is that okay?" Aliyah asked, reminding her mother of why she dropped by.

"Yes, yes, of course," her mother said, shooing her off. "Wait, are you going to wear *that* to lunch with Connie?"

"Yes," Aliyah said, trying to make it to her car. Her outfit was simple. Beige knee-length shorts and a starched white t-shirt—unacceptable to her mother beyond the house. The flip-flops, no matter how fashionable, were almost too much to bear.

"I know I have something in my closet that will fit you. Why don't you check?" she said, not really asking.

"I'm wearing this, Mom."

"But honey, this is a major television personality. You should fix yourself up better. The ladies do talk you know."

"I'm wearing this," she said, making her escape before her mother dragged her into the house for an unwanted makeover.

Oriental teas in a beautifully decorated box with Japanese inscriptions that Lena couldn't read—this was Connie's contribution to the meal.

"You did say you were cooking oriental didn't you?" Connie asked rhetorically as she walked into the house and presented her with the package.

"I brought fortune cookies," Aliyah spoke up, walking in behind her. "They're gourmet."

"Thanks," Lena said, amused.

The ladies picked at their food. Connie and Aliyah studied the colorful specks of tough meat peeking out from a mound of fried rice. It wasn't very good. Lena knew it.

"Is this rib meat?" Aliyah asked curiously.

"Yes," Lena said, under the mistaken impression that a compliment would follow.

Connie sat her plate down and raised her eyebrows at Lena.

"All I can say is it's a good thing you didn't make this for the first meal you cooked for us."

Lena lowered her eyes feeling the weight of her humiliation. Connie gently touched her arm.

"I guess that will teach me to open my big mouth and complain about good old fashioned home cooking."

"Amen," Aliyah added.

They all looked at each other, and then burst into unexpected laughter. The usual tension in the room was lifted.

"Sister, I think this is about the worst forkful of food I've had in a long time," Connie said in between gasps for breath.

"Maybe I can whip us up a burger or something," Lena said optimistically.

"Don't worry about it. This is my fault and I have just what we need to wash this meal down." Connie reached into her purse and pulled out a small gold flask. "A drink," she said as she poured a little into their teacups.

"Is that alcohol?" Lena timidly asked.

"It most definitely is," Connie said.

Lena and Aliyah sat in stunned silence.

"Ladies, don't look so afraid. Jesus drank wine for goodness' sake," she said. "Take a sip; you'll like it."

Lena decided to pass, afraid of what the Pastor would say if he came home and smelled alcohol on her breath. He didn't like alcohol. He'd seen its uncontrollable power over people in his family and warned Lena about awakening that demon.

Aliyah hadn't had a drink since she and Jay broke up. He always offered her a taste of whatever exotic mixed drink he had, but he never let her get drunk, except for that one time.

"You've had enough," Jay said as he pried the drink from Aliyah's hands. She was giggly, laughing at nothing and everything.

"More!" she demanded of the fruit-flavored drink she had clearly forgotten was full of alcohol. She'd been stealing sips from his glass, drinking too fast, and feeling the effects even faster.

"No," he said sternly, pouring the drink into an already dead potted plant.

She danced to the demo he was playing for her in his studio, her short skirt rising with every move. Jay sat immobilized as she climbed onto his lap and kissed him.

"I love you," she said, pulling off her shirt and revealing

a soft pink lace bra that told of her innocence. He could have had her if he wanted, but she was worth more than a ride on a worn leather couch in a music studio.

"I love you, too," he said, meaning it for the first time in his life. "That's why I'm taking you home."

Aliyah took a long sip of the spirited tea. It eased down the back of her throat and tickled like tiny spider legs then landed with an unusual bite she wasn't prepared for. She coughed most of it back up. Composing herself, she quickly put the cup back to her lips, letting the liquid enter her mouth slowly this time, and managed to hold it down. She held out her cup for more. Connie smiled and nodded approval.

"So, Miss Lena, tell us a little something about yourself," Connie said unexpectedly.

Lena wasn't sure how much Connie really wanted to know. It wasn't like FLS hadn't already done a thorough background check. Her mother said the membership committee even called and interviewed her over the telephone, making her question even more why Lena wanted to be a part of such a "pretentious" group.

"I guess you can tell I love to cook," she said. "You can thank my grandmother for all the foods you've enjoyed because she taught me everything I know about cooking. Well, except this food today. I can't put that on her."

Connie and Aliyah laughed hard—in no small part

thanks to the two cups of tea they'd already had.

"I was raised in Lincoln County, just a few hours from here."

"You're from around here?" Aliyah asked, not realizing it until now and confirming Lena's suspicion that neither she nor Connie had even bothered to read the brief bio she submitted with her membership application. "Where did you go to school?"

There was only one school. "Lincoln County High School," Lena answered.

Aliyah let out a surprisingly girlish giggle. "Our big rivals! I went to Martindale."

Lena knew exactly where she'd gone to school and it might as well have been on the other side of the earth. Lincoln County was one of the poorest areas in the state. By contrast Martindale was one of the richest, with most of the families like Aliyah's settling in the even more affluent pockets of Chestnut Falls. Growing up, Lena was all too aware that her situation was better than most of her Lincoln County classmates because of the choices and effort her family put into giving her more options. Her mother was educated and got a job teaching at the elementary school. Her grandparents left the city, bought acres of farmland, raised hogs, and opened the county's first sausage plant. And then there was her father, Stanley. But she decided not to mention him. Some things were better kept private.

The only time Martindale students crossed paths

with students from Lincoln County was at the annual football playoffs. Lincoln County was always the winner. They had to be. The ability to play sports was usually their only legal ticket out of a rural, impoverished existence.

"Different field, different master, same old slavery," *Richard often smirked from the bleachers as the players* *ran up and down the practice field. He'd just finished* *reading* The Autobiography of Malcolm X *and prided* *himself on being more enlightened than anyone else.* *Still, they went to every game and he would sit on his* *makeshift throne and make patronizing comments. But* *when their team was losing, he would get quiet and fidget,* *trying unsuccessfully not to look at the scoreboard.*

All the coaches watched him in P.E. and tried to coax *him into trying out for the team—any team. He was tall* *enough to own the basketball court and strong enough to* *command attention on the football field. But he refused* *to "be paraded around like chattel for the man."*

"Less than sixty percent of our students graduate. *Some of them can't even spell football. I'll join the team* *when they deal with that," he argued like an old soul. But* *in a strange way, Lena felt like he was really more afraid of* *failing than anything else.*

"My husband and I were high school sweethearts and have been married for almost six years."

"Married six years," Connie said amazed. "You must have been babies when you married."

"Right out of high school," she said sheepishly.

Connie offered Aliyah more to drink. She'd forgotten how much more fun it was to drink with someone. "Well, if you've been married for six years don't you think it's about time for some babies around here?"

"I hope so. With the new church and everything, he's not sure . . . ," Lena hesitated. "We're not sure if the time is right."

"The time is never really right," Aliyah spoke up.

Connie didn't ask any more questions, but she obviously was in no hurry to leave, and neither was Aliyah.

"Do either of you play cards?" Lena asked after a few seconds of trying to come up with a new topic for conversation.

"A little bridge, but I'm not very good," Connie said.

"I'm afraid I can't play anything. I don't think I've seen a deck of cards since college," Aliyah admitted.

"How about Scrabble? I've got a board upstairs," Lena offered.

"Scrabble is good. I think I can still spell," Aliyah said, welcoming the chance to kill some time to let any odor of alcohol wear off her breath. "How about you Miss TV personality? Can you spell?" she asked playfully.

For grown women—church first ladies no less— to sit around playing a board game seemed absurd on the surface, but Connie was in no mood to go home to a big empty house, and Scrabble certainly was more dignified than passing around a pint of bourbon.

"I guess you're about to find out," Connie said, rising to the challenge.

Lena skipped triumphantly up the stairs to retrieve the game. She'd won them over with a bad meal and a board game. If only she'd known it was so easy.

The irritation seeping from her mother was obvious when Aliyah arrived to pick up Jeremiah. With the baby in one arm and her other hand on her hip, she looked accusingly at the clock.

"Hi, Mom. Sorry I'm a little late," she said as she scooped the exhausted infant out of her mother's arms.

"Late? You call this a *little* late? It's six o'clock. I had to cancel my dinner plans," her mother scolded.

"I'm sorry. I don't know where the time went. Sister Connie had a lot to talk about," she said in an attempt to temper her mood. "We're trying to get Lena ready to be an official FLS member. You don't want anybody making *your* organization look bad do you?"

Her mother's lips curled. She moved closer, suspicious of the lightness in her walk.

"From the smell of things you were doing more than getting this woman prepared for FLS."

Aliyah had meant to pick up some chewing gum on her way. Her mother had a nose like a bloodhound, and even though she'd stopped drinking hours earlier her mother could smell it.

"It's just a little . . . ," she stopped short of explaining any further, trying instead to put a more comfortable distance between them.

"Foolish, foolish, foolish," her mother said sharply over one of her famously chastising glares. "You have to be more aware of the devil . . . more aware than ever before. You know what's at stake."

"Everything is under control, Mom."

"So said Eve when she took a bite of the fruit."

"Look, I'm sorry I was late. It won't happen again. I'll get a sitter for Jeremiah next week," she said sighing and gathering up his things.

"Oh, please. Stop being dramatic. You know I'll watch my precious grandson anytime. But no more drinking, and call if you're going to be late, and . . ."

"Thanks, Mom," Aliyah interrupted before her mother could give any more directives.

Aliyah lay in bed watching the minutes flip by on the digital clock. 11:00. That was late even for the Reverend. She was surprised to find herself waiting up for him or even thinking that he might want to talk. She had become a master of talking to herself, rambling on and on and waiting pointlessly for a response from his side of the bed. She swore sometimes he faked snoring.

When she heard the garage door open, she turned off the light, rolled over, and pulled up the covers. She decided to save herself the frustration of having a one-way conversation.

The Reverend was worn out when he made it home from the cross-country campaign. He'd secured the votes he needed, but the trip had drained and disappointed him. He'd told Aliyah and the Council that he wanted to be presiding bishop to share the gospel and move the church forward. His genuineness had touched her in a strange way. But, with the official election looming, he was discovering that not everyone shared his motivation.

Designers and decorators had invaded the church armed with renovation plans for a building committee he didn't remember appointing. The presiding bishop's church was supposed to look a certain way. Everyone agreed that the church had to keep its historical feel in homage to Aliyah's grandfather and father, but modern touches would signal a new era not just at the church but for the entire council membership.

"Your job is to make us strong again—the envy of all denominations," one advisor unashamedly told him.

And he was receiving an onslaught of unsolicited advice about imposing new rules for the sanctuary. No young children. No feeding babies. No chewing gum. No walking. No talking. After all, the country would be watching his church and following his lead if done right.

The Reverend was learning, just as Aliyah's father had, that being the leader meant compromise. Sometimes you do what God wants. Most of the time, you do what the people demand.

Chapter 11

Lena stood at the door of their study, waiting for the Pastor to notice her. He grunted as he sifted through the numerous messages on his desk. Lena had started sorting his messages in categories of urgent and not so urgent—most were from church members he never seemed to have enough time for anymore; some were reporters wanting interviews; others were names Lena didn't recognize—not that the Pastor returned any of the calls any faster.

After a few seconds, she cleared her throat to get his attention.

"Are you busy?" she asked, startling him.

"Never too busy for my beautiful wife," he said.

"How's everything going?" she asked timidly. "The church is okay?"

Pastor leaned back in his chair and propped his

hands on his head. "Nothing for you to worry about. Things are fine."

"Are we okay?" she asked, crossing the room to stand in front of him.

He rose from his chair and pulled her to him. He slowly kissed her as he held her face in his hands. She held on to him tightly, afraid to let go.

"You tell me?" he smiled and pulled her onto his lap. He tickled her until her cream colored cheeks turned red from laughter.

"Maybe we should continue this in the bedroom," she suggested, pulling him closer, but not in time to beat the telephone.

"Can't you let it ring just once?" she pleaded as he reached for it.

Pastor nervously looked at his watch. The strain on his face told her he had to answer it. He picked up the receiver and cupped his hand over the mouthpiece.

"Why don't you go upstairs and wait for me. I'll just be a few minutes," he whispered. He blew her a kiss as she walked out. "Shut the door please."

Lena closed the door, but left a small crack. She stood quietly listening. Her husband's voice was so low and muffled that she had to strain to make out what he was saying.

"I'm going to tell you one last time to stop calling my house. I told you I'd meet you later tonight and I will," he said, between his teeth. "I'll be there when I get there. You know my wife is here. I can't just up and leave and that's that."

Pastor slammed down the phone. Lena tipped away from the door and quickly crept upstairs.

"Who was that on the phone?" she asked when he walked into the bedroom. Without answering he kissed her, unzipped her dress, and let it fall to the floor.

"I love you," he said, wedging her body underneath his.

Even as they lay in bed together with his arms draped around her, Lena knew that everything was not okay.

"What exactly is N-I-T supposed to be?" Connie skeptically asked Lena while chomping on a turkey sandwich. Lena had nothing left to prove. She could cook, set a table, and recite the FLS bylaws from memory, so Connie and Aliyah didn't say a word when she pulled a deli tray from the refrigerator.

"Nit. You know, like nit knack," Aliyah defended.

"I believe that's knick knack my dear," Connie corrected.

"I'm sure it's a word. Do you want to challenge me?" she said, calling her bluff with a poker face fit for a Las Vegas card shark.

Connie looked at the scorecards. She was in last

place as always, one of the drawbacks of having every written document prepared for you by publicists and scriptwriters. That she still knew how to spell anything was a miracle. But she tossed Aliyah's creation around in her head for a few seconds certain it wasn't a real word.

"Lena, get the dictionary," she said, feeling victorious.

Lena robotically scanned each page of the dictionary.

"Nit: the egg or young of a parasitic insect such as a louse," she recited as a teacher introducing a new unimportant word to her class.

"Ha! Rack up my points, sister," Aliyah said with an exuberance that surprised even her.

Connie shook her head in disbelief and waited for a sideline cheer from Lena. When Lena failed to join in Aliyah's celebration, Connie asked, "Are you okay?"

"I'm just a little tired," Lena said softly, secretly hoping the game would end soon.

Connie and Aliyah gave understanding nods. Lena was moving full force into the life of a pastor's wife. She'd have many sleepless nights. But they sensed more was wrong than just sleep deprivation.

"Are you sure there's nothing wrong?" Aliyah asked.

Lena wanted to say no. She wasn't sure about anything anymore.

"Do you think true men of God cheat on their wives?" she answered Aliyah with a question.

"You're kidding right?" Connie snickered, not giving Aliyah time to answer. Lena's expression told her otherwise. *Poor girl,* Connie thought, *she really is naïve.* Because of her connections and the length of time she'd spent in the inner sanctum of this world, Connie had amassed an exhaustive list of "men of God" who had been unfaithful. Some had been publicly exposed. Others still had their secrets well protected.

The Bishop's young assistant adjusted her clothes and pulled her hair back into a high ponytail before slipping out of his dressing room. From behind a curtain on the darkened set, Connie secretly watched her emerge with an armful of papers that were supposedly script changes, production material, and mail.

The Bishop was still in his boxer shorts when Connie stormed into his dressing room with a fist full of her own papers. "This is evidence," she snarled waving them in his face, "the kind of evidence that could ruin everything we've worked for." She angrily tossed credit card receipts she'd found for clothing and jewelry at him. He stood with a blank stare as if surprised she'd figured out what was going on right under her nose. He hadn't taken the time to script a lie for a moment like this. He didn't need to bother. Connie already had an explanation ready for him.

"You obviously bought these things for me and someone is just holding them until you're ready to surprise me with them. And I think you're ready now. So

you can either tell someone to bring me my things or you will be paying for a whole lot more than some trifling little presents," she threatened.

Connie took a deep breath and ripped up the receipts, leaving the scraps on the floor.

Connie remembered when the woman, barely out of her teens, walked into their lives over a year ago. She sauntered into the Bishop's office, her long shapely legs, tanned and slathered in baby oil, greeting him first—a college student in need of a job, she said. He hired her on the spot. No resume. No questions about whether she was even a Christian. It took only a few weeks for her to become indispensable to him.

Connie was almost sincere when she told herself that she didn't care anymore.

"I'm sorry. Really. I didn't mean to laugh," Connie said, composing herself. "Honey, all men have the capacity to cheat. Godly men just don't do it well."

"Don't listen to her," Aliyah said, unsure of where this conversation was going.

In the silence that followed, Lena could feel the burning question hanging in the air. They wanted to know if her husband was having an affair. She could speculate and tell them yes, ruining her husband's reputation and her chance of becoming an FLS member. Then again she could go with her heart, and her heart just couldn't believe that the Pastor would do such a thing.

"Well, thank the Lord I don't have to worry about that," she said, managing to pull a smile together.

That a girl, Connie mused, *learn to lie to yourself.*

Godly men don't cheat well. If Connie were right, Lena would find some evidence of another woman carelessly left behind by the Pastor.

A search of his pants pockets turned up a handful of lint, some loose change, and a few peppermints. It was about the same for his coat pockets. She also checked his wallet while he was in the shower. She didn't know what she expected to find—a mysterious phone number, love note, photograph—but found nothing suspicious.

The only thing she'd left untouched was his study. It had never been off limits, but she'd never had much reason to go in there, at least not while he wasn't home. She stood at the door, uncertain about going in and rummaging through the mountain of mess that covered his desk. She pictured Stan's wife doing as much through the course of their marriage.

Lena had never given Stan's wife or their family much thought. They were all anonymous to her and Stan had never pushed for a family gathering. But as a wife herself, hoping and praying against the existence of another woman, she now imagined how his wife must have felt knowing without a doubt that Lena and her mother were quite real and knowing that she had to share her bed and her life with someone else. She pitied his wife and her mother for accepting Stan's terms.

Lena flipped through the stacks of letters, bills, and miscellaneous papers on the Pastor's desk. Nothing was out of the ordinary. Each drawer she opened was filled with normal office things—supplies, sermon notes, and files—except for the one she couldn't open. The desk was old, a bargain she'd found at the local Goodwill, and the drawers were prone to sticking. She pulled harder, thinking the drawer had gotten off track. But it wouldn't budge. Beneath the tarnished brass handle, she noticed a small keyhole. Maybe the drawer was locked. But it was just the two of them; there was no need to lock anything. She sat behind his desk, staring at the drawer, and thinking of ways to open it, but unsure if she really wanted to know what was inside.

"You've got to learn to sit up straight," Connie admonished Lena.

"Yes, we don't want Jesus to come back on Judgment Day and catch you with slumped shoulders," Aliyah chimed in jokingly.

First ladies are to exude a certain air of self-confidence; it's expected, Aliyah's mother had told her. FLS first ladies carry themselves like royalty by right and through proper training. They remain humble and committed to their godly subjects, but there is no mistaking the first lady of the church. She either wears the biggest hat, sits in the seat closest to the pulpit, has the most sequins on her suit, or simply has an unmistakable sense of righteousness. The difference between Aliyah and Lena was that while Aliyah simply despised the pretentiousness of church protocol, Lena was too unsure of herself to pull it off successfully. Choosing not to accept the role of first lady and being too afraid to take your place were two very different things. If the church sensed fear, the congregation would walk all over her. Connie knew it too.

"Have you ever straightened your hair?" Connie asked out of the blue. She'd been polishing a few pieces of silver she was loaning Lena for when she hosted the executive committee for lunch, something expected of each candidate. Lena had been completely surprised by Connie's gesture.

Lena brushed her hand along her slicked back ponytail. Her wild mane, a curse from her mother's union with Stan, always irritated her. She kept it pulled up unless the Pastor pleaded with her to let it down, usually at night.

"Be proud of your uniqueness," he'd told her.

"No, I never have," she said.

Connie snapped off her latex gloves and set the

silver along the kitchen counter to dry. She held Lena's face in her hand before pulling her hair from the rubber band. Large blond waves fell down her back. She had even more hair than Connie imagined.

"I need a blow dryer, hair pins, and a brush," she instructed Lena.

"You know how to do hair?" Aliyah quizzed skeptically.

"The Bishop and I didn't always have a $10 million studio and a staff you know. We started out on public access television and we had to do everything ourselves—hair, makeup, wardrobe. I got pretty good."

Connie dragged her victim up to the bathroom where Lena dug through her drawers and dutifully handed over the requested tools. Connie went to work, pulling and yanking Lena's hair in every direction, taking control of the rebellious curls.

"Head up. Head down," Connie ordered, never giving Lena time to obey, but moving it where she wanted it to go. Smoke was rising from the blow dryer, and a few times Connie scraped her ear with the rapidly moving brush.

There was a reason Lena had never tried this before.

When Connie finished, she dug through her purse for her compact, dusted Lena's face with powder, gave her a few squirts of hair spray, and presented her to the bathroom mirror. Lena was amazed at the woman staring back at her. A smile spread across her face.

"I like it," she said beaming.

"That makes two of us," Aliyah said, applauding the transformation. Connie looked at her as if to let her know she was next.

Four hang ups in one-hour. Lena had counted. Whoever was calling her house at midnight didn't want to speak to her. Maybe the caller didn't want to speak to anybody, but merely enjoyed annoying and disturbing unsuspecting sleepers. Not that Lena had shut her eyes all night. Pastor had been gone since the morning, not even bothering to tell her goodbye. She called the church and he was out. She tried later and only got his voice mail. His cell phone was turned off too. She thought about calling some of the church leaders, the few he'd kept, to ask if they'd seen him. But she decided there was no need in worrying them or giving them something to gossip about.

Had FLS driven a wedge between them? She could give it up. Sitting up straight, crossing her legs the right way, and properly positioning herself beside her husband—not behind, but not directly beside—she was questioning what it all meant anyway, even though it seemed so clear before. The mystique of the elite was waning. It had become obvious that money, a well-respected name, and club membership couldn't shield you from life's problems.

Or was the wedge a *somebody?* She stared at the ceiling and prayed.

Chapter 12

Six weeks had passed without thought. Spring was surrendering to summer, and in less than two weeks Lena would join the FLS sisterhood officially. Today Connie was helping her master the art of draping a modesty cloth over her legs.

"It serves no purpose if your legs aren't crossed at the ankle," Connie critiqued.

With the time winding down, Lena should have been nervous, anxious even. But her mind clearly was elsewhere.

"Okay, what's going on?" Connie finally asked, growing frustrated at Lena's inability to follow simple directives.

Lena fiddled with the cloth, trying to control and distinguish the sensible thoughts from the irrational ones that were racing through her head. The Pastor loved her. She loved him. Nothing—no one—could possibly come between them.

"When did you know you'd found the love of your life?" Lena asked quietly.

"I'm still looking," Connie teased. "Really, I'm too old to remember. I'll let Sister Aliyah answer that one."

Aliyah looked up from the pile of slipcovers she was considering for Lena's worn sofa. When did she know she'd found the love of her life? She was unsure if she should tell the uncomfortable truth or a respectable lie. *You have to be more aware of the devil, more aware than ever before. You know what's at stake,* she could hear her mother saying.

"When even after that person has made you cry more than you ever have in your life and left a gaping hole in your heart, there's no one else whose voice, touch, or kiss will ever make you feel so alive." Aliyah had never spoken out loud what she felt, never been able to wrap her mind around it herself. Hearing her voice speak the truth was liberating.

"I married my husband because he was safe," she went on. "I was in love with another man . . . before him. His name was Jay. He goes by J. Prince now."

"Wait, you don't mean J. Prince, the award winning, multi-millionaire singer!" Lena exclaimed, almost jumping out of her chair and sending her modesty cloth to the floor. Aliyah nodded and placed it back on her lap.

"Oh my gosh! I love his music. I mean . . . I used to. Okay, I still do," she said with more excitement than she'd exhibited all day. "Do you know how many babies his songs are responsible for?" She rattled off a list of his songs as if Aliyah didn't know them all. Aliyah had demos he'd given her—music he'd never recorded or released. It was too bad she'd thrown them away along with every photo they'd ever taken together.

Connie finally chuckled, convinced Aliyah was joking. "There's no need in teasing this poor child."

"I'm not," Aliyah said firmly. "I met him in a club years ago. We dated for a year and even talked about getting married."

"Really? What happened?" Lena asked anxiously.

"He got his big break, went on the road, and forgot all about this little Miss Nobody."

Connie didn't like hearing Aliyah refer to herself as a nobody, especially when it was a man making her feel that way. "Sounds like you have some words for this J. Prince" she said.

Aliyah shrugged, surprised she was even talking about him to anyone.

"Well, I'm not supposed to tell anyone, but we are trying to book him for our show," Connie said.

Aliyah froze.

"We're thinking about start a celebrity Christian spotlight segment each month and he's on our wish list. We've been hearing he's a new convert to Christ with a powerful testimony. If we land him, I can make sure you're right there."

Aliyah remembered the last time she almost came face to face with Jay. Jeremiah had been crying all day. He only stopped when she put him in the car and started driving. She wasn't sure how she'd ended up two hours away from home, parked in front of Atlantic City's Boardwalk Hall staring at Jay's name sprawled across the marquee.

The doors to the concert hall hadn't opened yet, but a crowd wound around the Grecian structure swaying anxiously and trying to keep warm in the wintery night air. Aliyah drove to the back toward a delivery area. She knew from the months of following Jay around when he was just the opening act that there was always a hidden door the performers used. She kept the car running but shut off her headlights and watched as three cars with black tinted windows pulled into the docking area. A man dressed in a dark coat and cap hustled to the passenger side of the first car. A long bare leg inched out as the driver extended his hand to a tall beautiful woman draped in a fur coat. Behind her was a man in sunglasses with the collar of his coat hiked around his ears. It was Jay. They rushed inside, arm and arm, with the rest of the entourage filing in behind them.

Aliyah pressed her head against the steering wheel. What had she thought—that she could just pick up and run away with him? A warm string of tears rolled down her chin and she was jarred by a sudden banging on her windshield.

"Hey lady, you can't park here!" a burly man yelled through the window. "You've got to move your car," he demanded before hitting her window again.

The sudden noise woke Jeremiah and he was wailing in the backseat. Aliyah shot the car in reverse and sped away.

"He probably wouldn't even remember me," she finally managed to say.

"Make him remember you," Connie retorted. "Let him see what a great woman he tossed aside. Maybe I'll make you a surprise guest."

"You wouldn't!" Aliyah said, jolted by the mere suggestion.

"Calm down, I'm kidding," Connie laughed. "My husband is persistent, but who knows if his people will even return our calls."

"Oh this is so romantic," Lena squealed, before running to the bathroom to hug the toilet.

The walls of the house vibrated the way they sometimes did during a storm, and the thunderous boom of music lured Lena to the window. A blue and gold-trimmed

Cadillac pulled into her driveway and a giant of a man emerged wearing enough gold chains to sink himself in the ocean. He walked with a cocky swagger toward her house not bothering to turn the car or the music off or to introduce himself when Lena cautiously opened the door.

"I'm looking for the preacher man," he said, lowering his sunglasses and looking past her and into the house.

"Pastor Richard isn't here," she purposely corrected.

The man waited, deciding for himself whether to take her word for it and leave. He lit a cigarette and let his eyes travel as far back into the house as they could without saying a word. He kept the smoke in his mouth, never exhaling.

She closed the door slightly, trying to wedge herself between him and a clear view of her living room.

"Can I help you with something?"

"Yeah, tell preacher man that Blue came by."

Blue? She'd never heard him mention anyone by that name. He couldn't be a church member. She would have remembered someone like him.

"Mr. Blue, what do you want with my husband?"

"You just tell him I was here and hopefully he'll take care of his business so that you won't have to worry your pretty little head about what I want with him."

Lena's uneasiness gave way to irritation. "I'll worry about my pretty little head, thank you. Now what can my husband do for you?"

He smirked, took a long slow drag of his cigarette, and flicked it in her yard. He moved in closer, testing her bravado. She didn't move. She couldn't move.

"Let's just say I'm an investor in God's kingdom and I'm expecting my tenfold return as promised." He turned, went back to his car, and drove away, his music echoing through the neighborhood long after he disappeared from sight.

Lena braced herself against the door to keep from falling. She needed to throw up but her throat was tightening, making her feel even worse. She felt her legs failing. She couldn't breath. Then the room went black.

"Sweetheart, are you okay? Baby, can you hear me?" Pastor asked nervously. He was sitting beside Lena's outstretched body on the sofa and had placed a cool towel on her forehead. She slowly opened her eyes. His face was filled with worry as he reached to embrace her.

"What happened? I found you on the floor? You had me so scared. Should I call the doctor?" He leaned in to kiss her. She coldly turned away.

"Your friend Blue dropped by," Lena said, finding her voice. She braced herself for the Pastor's response, but he was quiet, perhaps hoping she wouldn't ask the next obvious question. She sat up, trying to steady herself.

"Who is he?"

Pastor Richard stood up and turned his back to her.

"A brother from my old neighborhood in Chicago," he answered. He hoped that would be enough to satisfy her, and there was a time when Lena would have accepted that as a sufficient answer. But for weeks he'd sensed a shift in his wife. She was more confident, more independent, a critical thinker. Until now, that's what he'd been praying for.

"Why is he looking for you?" she demanded.

He didn't want to lie to her.

"Let's talk about this later, when you're feeling better," he suggested.

Lena's head was throbbing and she didn't know if and when she'd have to race to the bathroom.

"You probably won't be here later," she said, resolved not to close the door on the conversation. "Just tell me straight. Who is he and why did he come stomping up to our front door today, demanding to see you?"

Pastor Richard held his breath. For months he'd deluded himself into believing that he could keep his misdeeds from Lena, from everyone, forever.

"I owe him some money," he confessed, barely above a whisper.

"How much?"

Pastor let out a heavy sigh. "Eighty thousand dollars."

"Eighty thousand dollars!" She thought about Blue's car, gaudy jewelry, and the cocky way he walked up to her house. "Eighty thousand dollars," she repeated, as if saying it again would change something.

"Where does a man like Blue get eighty thousand dollars to just give away?" she asked. Pastor's guilt-ridden expression told her what she already knew.

"Why did you need his money?" she fired off. Maybe if she got mad enough she would wake up from this nightmare.

"To finish work on the church."

"We had a loan."

"They wouldn't lend us the full amount we asked for and I wasn't going to be able to get everything we'd shown the congregation. I couldn't fail them or God."

A lump was forming in her throat. She pushed it down, forcing another question.

"How were you going to pay him back?"

"We had an arrangement."

"What kind of arrangement?" she asked, terrified of the answer.

Pastor didn't want to answer any more questions. All of his answers were things Lena didn't want to hear, things he never wanted her to hear.

"I gave him a percentage off the top from our weekly offerings, with a little added interest."

Lena's chest was burning. Every breath took effort and her legs felt like they were going to give out again.

"I thought with all the publicity, having three services, and us being filled to capacity each Sunday, I'd have him paid off in a month. But we're barely bringing in enough to pay back the bank on time each month."

As ashamed as he was, the heavy weight of the lies he'd been carrying was falling from his shoulders. Even though he could feel Lena's anger rising, it felt good to finally tell somebody what was going on. He had kept the burdensome secret much longer than he'd ever planned.

Maybe his grandparents were right—the path of life is circular. There was no other way to explain how he and Blue ended up in the same city thousands of miles from the Chicago housing project where they'd played together as boys. But there he was standing on the corner pretending to be doing nothing while the Pastor was handing out church flyers. The last time he'd seen Blue he was in the back of a police car, bloodied and bruised and headed to juvenile detention. Pastor might have been with him if he hadn't decided to skip the liquor store robbery and go to a youth Bible study instead. His mother had been gone for two days, feeding her drug habit in the skeletal remains of some long-abandoned building. He was hungry and he'd only gone to the church for the free pizza. He was as surprised as anyone when the choir's song stirred him to give his life to Christ. When he watched Blue being hauled off like a captured animal, he knew God had rescued him.

That was over ten years ago, right before he was sent to live with his grandmother in Chestnut Falls. He assumed Blue was dead by now or serving harder time somewhere. He wasn't sure if Blue saw him and decided against an impromptu reunion until the day he needed him.

Blue's hangout was a local downtown club known for growing music superstars back in the day. Now it was a different sort of place. Even in the hazy, smoke-filled room, Blue was easy to spot. His secluded table was the one surrounded by a menacing entourage and nearly naked women panting for a minute of his attention. Pastor Richard walked confidently toward the table and was immediately met by two young men who stood within inches of Blue, drawing discreet attention to the bulges in their jackets. They stopped short of putting their hands on him, maybe because he stared them down like he'd done many times in the old neighborhood, identifying himself as a retired yet still capable member of their secret fraternity. Also because Blue caught a glimpse of his face through the cigarette smoke and motioned him past his protectors.

"Preacher man!" he said, with more excitement than Pastor expected. "Man, how long has it been?"

They exchanged a street handshake and a manly pat on the back. Pastor was relieved that his old friend remembered him. Blue signaled the waitress for a round of drinks and made room for Pastor between him and one of his female companions. She gave Pastor Richard *an inviting eye, telling him she was available if he were willing. He wasn't.*

"Don't start messing with this man or you could go up in flames," Blue teased the woman. "Everybody, this is an old friend of mine, the one and only and very esteemed Pastor of Friendship Community Baptist Church. You know, the church that has been luring away some of our best business associates and customers," Blue announced with a touch of sarcasm that Pastor Richard didn't appreciate. Blue knew he had offended him.

"I'm just messing with you man. Really it's good to see you. What brings you to my joint? You know I own this place now, right?"

Pastor Richard studied the faces at the table and looked at Blue. He wanted to talk alone. Blue caught on quickly. He snapped his fingers and, amidst moans and groans, everyone dispersed.

"What's going on?" Blue asked, intrigued.

"I need a favor."

Lena was eerily quiet. It was all beginning to make sense to her now—why he had begun thumping his chest from the pulpit, why he'd begun proclaiming himself a spiritual dictator, and why he'd given himself exclusive access to the church account, disempowered the trustee board, and kept only the few deacons who pledged unequivocal loyalty to him. But, the church membership was growing by leaps and bounds and he'd delivered on his promises. They opened a community grocery store, a daily soup kitchen that distributed meals to the hungry, and a clothes closet for the needy. He was doing what most preachers only talked about. Yet, he'd become as corrupt as the ones he'd grown up despising. He'd made a deal with the devil *for* God.

"How could you possibly think you could pay back eighty thousand dollars in a month?"

"I only borrowed fifty, but when I fell behind on payments Blue wanted me to start doing some other jobs for him. When I refused, he hiked it up to eighty. Called it deferred interest."

"And if we don't have it?"

Blue didn't strike Lena as the type of man who would expose the Pastor. He wanted something else. Pastor's eyes fell away from Lena. He'd hoped she wouldn't ask that question. "If I don't pay him by the end of the month, he cashes in the collateral—the deed to our house," he said just above a whisper.

The only real thing they had to call their own was their house. They'd come across it at a tax sale—an old, forgotten house that had been abandoned generations ago. Nobody had bothered to pay taxes for years and the city wanted its money. Notices had been posted and Lena and the Pastor waited anxiously for someone to reclaim the lost treasure. When no one did, they drained their meager savings and got a small loan to make a sizeable bid. For $35,000, no warranties, no remodeling allowances, and no guarantees that the house wouldn't collapse at any time, the house was theirs.

Lena spent countless hours at yard sales, flea markets, and salvage stores. She reupholstered an old sofa and loveseat, made curtains, and refinished an antiquated dining room table all by herself. She painted, pulled up ragged carpet, and transformed their humble house into a home. This was *her* house. And it was all too obvious what a man like Blue would do with it.

Finally, the tears came. She fell into hysterical, uncontrollable sobbing filled with rage, fear, and pain. For the first time in her life, she hated the sight of her husband.

"Please, please don't cry," he pleaded and reached unsuccessfully for her. "I'm going to make it all right. I promise."

"You can't promise me anything anymore," she spat out. She ran upstairs and slammed the bedroom door, sending a painting crashing to the floor. She yanked the ringing telephone out of the wall.

Chestnut Falls, a whistle stop of a town, was still asleep when Lena pulled into her mother's gravel driveway. The crush of rock under her tires woke the dog that was sprawled out on the porch. She swore Sammy was the town's oldest dog. A mixed up breed of everything, she and her mother found him whimpering on the side of the road one summer day as they walked home from picking peaches.

"We should call her Peaches," her mother declared. Two days later they realized she was a he and renamed him Sammy. Half blind and looking like a big ball of dough, he raised his head and welcomed a scratch under his chin as Lena stepped over him and grabbed the door key from under the mat.

The smell of fresh brewing coffee already filled the house thanks to the automatic coffee maker Lena had gotten her mother for Christmas.

"Mama, are you up?" Lena whispered as she slowly opened her mother's bedroom door. "Mama?" she nudged her.

Her mother rubbed the sleep from her eyes and looked blankly at her for a moment as if she were a hallucination.

"Lena, baby, is that you? Are you all right? What are you doing here?" her mother asked one question right behind the other with concern in her voice.

"I just thought I'd come home and see you that's all," Lena said quietly.

Her mother looked at the clock. "At 5:00 in the morning? You sure you're all right?"

"Fine, Mama, I'm fine," she said. She climbed in bed beside her as she did when she was little, pulled the covers up to her ears, and let her head sink into the pillow. She didn't feel like talking or reliving her nightmare just yet.

"I'm just fine," she said again before drifting off to sleep.

Chapter 13

Aliyah stood looking in the mirror, inspecting her body and holding an inch of soft flesh between her thumb and index finger, searching for signs of the hourglass figure she once took for granted. It had been a long time since the Reverend had called her beautiful or since she had felt that way. She lay on the bathroom floor, pulling her knees to her chest and holding a labored crunch.

"One, two, three," she grunted, sweat collecting on her forehead. "Four, five, six." She made it to ten before she heard a faint knocking on the door.

"Jeremiah is crying," the Reverend interrupted.

She stretched out her legs, pulled her arms over her head, and let out a deep breath. Maybe she'd start again tomorrow.

The mood of the executive committee was festive. New member selection was generally a cause for celebration. At this point, most candidates sailed through the election process. The president would read each individual name, pausing for a motion to accept them, followed by a second and a majority vote. If there were a problem, their mentors would be called in for a closed-door session to discuss the best way to explain the rejection to the candidate. Connie and Aliyah hadn't expected to be called for such a meeting.

Connie adjusted her eyes and tried to lift her feet one at a time. They felt cemented to the floor. If she'd remembered the morning FLS meeting she wouldn't have drunk so much the night before. The aspirin she tossed back in the car hadn't kicked in and when the committee chair banged her wooden gavel the sound echoed like glass shattering in her head.

She sat coolly at the head table hidden behind dark sunglasses and a hat. Everyone knew better than to ask her to remove them. Word had spread quickly that the Mayor had tapped her and the Bishop to be the goodwill ambassadors for gospel music. The city had won its bid to host the nationally televised festival of choirs for the first time and he wanted local star power to help catapult the city deeper into the music and entertainment industry. As part of the deal, Connie and the Bishop were serving as hosts and executive producers, which meant they would control the spotlight.

One by one, the ladies came up to her and exchanged air kisses. Fortunately, she'd spent the night nursing a bottle of Vodka so she didn't carry that stale sweet alcohol odor that came with other liquors. Still she was thankful for the mints dancing in her mouth and the floral perfume she'd spritzed behind her ears.

The protocol committee chair called the meeting to order.

"Before we get started with our business, I think we all want to congratulate Sister Connie on the incredible new milestone in her ministry." The ladies politely applauded, unaware that Connie's eyes had drifted shut, and she had already tuned them out.

"Sisters, this is awkward and, as always, I hate to do this," the president said as Connie and Aliyah took their seats. "But we have a problem with Lena James's nomination."

They sat, bewildered, unable to imagine what Lena could have hidden from them. In the eight weeks they'd known her, they hadn't suspected any wrongdoing. The truth is, in the history of the organization only two candidates had ever been withdrawn after making it this far. One had been found in a compromising position with a deacon. The other had a son who apparently liked to go to nightclubs dressed as a woman. It wasn't that the women couldn't have any transgressions. They just had to be contained. If FLS was able to discover misconduct, they clearly lacked the wisdom or connections with the right people to avoid exposure.

"It's not her, per se, but her husband's church. The records just don't gel," she continued. "They have expenses of some $40,000 a month and only generate about $15,000."

"We checked their bank account," the secretary added. Connie always wondered how they pulled that off legally and what else they might have access to. "They're not sitting on a gold mine, but more money has to be coming from somewhere."

"You know we don't like secrets when it comes to money. That's just a disaster waiting to happen," the president rationalized. "We've even had problems pinning down her husband's actual salary."

"That's because he doesn't have one," Aliyah spoke up, feeling as though her silence was betraying her new friend. "He gets a Sunday stipend."

"Again, that's just not reflected in the books," the president said.

Connie knew where this was going and there was no point in fighting. Funny, nobody questioned the millions of dollars she and the Bishop took in each year or what they did with it.

"There are things we can and do overlook, but discrepancies in financial matters are not among those things. So we need to discuss how to notify her."

"I . . . ," Connie stopped herself and looked at Aliyah for a reassuring nod. "We want to be the ones to tell her." They knew Lena. If anything inappropriate was happening, she was oblivious.

They called her from Connie's dressing room, but got no answer. They left two more messages, imploring her to call them as soon as possible. By the third call, the answering machine didn't pick up.

Fifty choirs had auditioned for a slot in the gospel festival. The Bishop and Connie were responsible for picking out twenty of the most dynamically entertaining groups and producing a show that would be a ratings winner. This was their first foray into primetime television.

Connie stretched out on the sofa in the Bishop's office, drinking a soda doused with a splash of rum. She watched audition tapes with the volume turned down. She had decided that whichever choirs could draw her into the screen when she didn't even know what they were singing would get picked. The Bishop poured over storyboards that had been sent to them by prospective writers. He didn't like any of the ideas. He complained to Connie who was only half listening how they were too predictable and uninspired.

"We need someone big standing center stage when the lights come up to open the show with a medley of gospel hits and then the choirs rise up from beneath the floor as backup," he said as he doodled furiously on one of the storyboards. "What do you think?"

It had been a long time since they were in a room

together, talking and planning something. Usually the Bishop or his assistant just told her when and where to show up.

"Who do you think we could get?" she asked, turning her attention away from the television and suggesting a few high-profile gospel artists they knew.

"No, think bigger," he admonished. His excitement was escalating. "Think platinum-selling, Grammy-award-winning artist. Think superstar and newly converted Christian . . . J. Prince."

Connie coughed up a little of her cocktail.

"I know we talked about trying to get him for our monthly spotlight, but this is more important. We've got to bring our A-plus game," he told Connie, explaining that this one night could make or break their ministry. Success would mean exposure to millions of households and greater commercial sponsorship for their network. They would also get an opportunity to further brand themselves as the "it" couple of television ministry. Of course he was subtler in the way he framed it.

"We'll be walking into God's greater anointing. And I need you to focus."

Connie knew the Bishop could sell bacon to a vegan, but getting an artist like J. Prince would be masterful. For a moment she was proud and excited again to be his wife. He rushed out of the office toting his notes and calling down the hall for his assistant, and just that quickly, the moment was gone.

She picked up her drink and saluted him with her glass as the door closed.

"I'm not a holy roller and I'm not becoming a gospel artist," J. Prince immediately told the Bishop. It had taken him two weeks to get the singer and his handlers on the phone.

"And that's what makes you perfect for the show," he explained.

The Bishop had been pandering to self-proclaimed celebrity Christians for months now, trying to fill his program roster. Connie didn't know where he'd gotten the idea, but everyone was excited about it. He'd pitched it a year earlier, but most of the A-list entertainers he'd made contact with were reluctant, worried they'd be perceived as religious fanatics and alienate some of their fan base if they talked about Jesus too openly. But Jay, known to the music world as J. Prince, was one of a handful of stars who had at least accepted the Bishop's phone call.

He had boldly shared his beliefs and newfound relationship with God in a magazine article that had crowned him the year's sexiest singer. His new album was even going to feature a gospel track. With him by their side, the gospel choir prime time special would be a ratings monster.

To seal the deal, the Bishop offered to have him come on their broadcast the week of the show and promote his new project and world tour. "Trust me, there are a whole lot of Christians who love you and your music."

Jay strolled across the set in black jeans and a silk sequined black t-shirt that stretched perfectly over his muscles. A silver and diamond cross dangled from his neck. He was strikingly handsome. Most celebrities Connie met were surprisingly dull looking in person. Thunderous applause and shrieks exploded from the audience before he even opened his mouth. When he did speak, he gave a raw testimony that sounded surprisingly genuine.

"I was a dead man. I had just performed in front of thousands of screaming fans, was lying in bed between two women I'd just met backstage, and I felt more alone than I'd ever felt in my life. I got up and hopped in my car ready to end it all."

A hush fell over the entire studio, the audience hanging on his every word. Aliyah too. Connie had followed through on her threat/promise to reunite them at the show.

Connie took his hand. "Go on, brother," the Bishop gently prodded. His story was better than he or Connie had expected.

A despondent millionaire driving aimlessly across the state looking for the right spot to crash his Lamborghini is how he described himself. Drunk and high on painkillers, he ran out of gas in front of a church. Slumped in his seat he heard what sounded like a cross between squawking ducks and cats in heat screeching Amazing Grace to an out of tune piano. He laughed at the horrid rendition and washed down his last pills with a gulp of Vodka, figuring this was as good a place as any to die. When he woke up the next morning still alive, he stumbled into the church service hoping no one would recognize him.

"My head was swimming and the usher sat me right down front by the speakers and of course they were singing 'Amazing Grace.' I guess that was God's payback. "

The audience laughed. He was as charming as ever, Aliyah thought as she watched him from the side of the stage.

"I told God I needed Him and gave my life to Him that day. Later that week I sent the church a new piano and found out I was nominated for a Grammy."

"Look at God work!" the Bishop shouted. The audience was up on its feet, shouting amens and hallelujahs. When the show broke for a commercial Jay finally spotted Aliyah. Their eyes locked for a few seconds and she thought about leaving, but changed her mind. Jay scooted closer to the edge of his seat as if planning to get up only to be stopped by the camera man announcing, "And we're back in 5 . . . 4 . . . 3 . . . "

"So, is there a special Christian lady in your life right now?" the Bishop asked after the break.

"No, I'm looking for a date. Any takers?" he flirted with the audience. "Seriously, I had a good woman once, but I lost her. I guess it was God's way of telling me I wasn't ready for one of His princesses."

Passionate sighs echoed through the studio. He had them in the palm of his hand. From the stage wing, Aliyah rolled her eyes. The drugs and alcohol must have affected his memory she decided. He didn't lose her; he left her.

"Keep serving the Lord son and maybe He'll bring her back to you," the Bishop said.

"He does work in mysterious ways," Jay acknowledged, trying to track Aliyah in his peripheral vision.

"Now, you are not only on tour for your new album, you have graciously agreed to headline the festival of choirs we are hosting tomorrow night," the Bishop inserted, smoothly shifting to the real reason for his appearance.

"That's right. My new album even features a gospel song. I have always loved inspirational music, and this is a really exciting opportunity to revisit my roots a little."

"Well, be sure to tune in tomorrow night for our national broadcast of the festival starting at 8:00 p.m."

Before closing in prayer, Connie and the Bishop surprised a few lucky audience members with free tickets to Jay's show and everyone received a copy of his new CD. When the interview wrapped, Jay's people whisked him backstage and almost past Aliyah.

"I'm cool," he said, breaking free. "Aliyah?" he called out in disbelief. He walked over toward her. "It's you for real?"

"In the flesh," she said sheepishly. *God please don't let him notice my droopy breasts and saggy butt,* she prayed, as if God would entertain such a request.

"I don't believe it. I really don't believe it."

She wondered what exactly he didn't believe—that she'd come to the studio to see him like a silly schoolgirl or that she'd become such a shell of the woman he once knew.

"You know I would have called if I wasn't so afraid of your Mom," he said, half joking. "My heart also couldn't take getting dissed again."

"Right, I dissed you," Aliyah said with a slight sarcastic edge in her voice.

"Well, a man can only take so many unanswered letters before he gives up, and when your Mom told me you were getting married, I knew I'd lost."

"Letters?" Aliyah asked, almost in a whisper of bewilderment.

"They meant that much to you, huh," he laughed.

"J.P. we really have to go man," a burly man whined.

"Okay, okay," he said. "Listen, I've got some radio stuff to do and a couple more interviews, but maybe we can grab some dinner or something; say around 8:30? I'm staying downtown." He hesitated. "Bring the husband. I'd like to meet the lucky man who stole my girl."

He wrote down his information and handed it to her before being rushed out of the building and into a waiting limousine.

"Where are the letters?" Aliyah demanded as she stormed into her mother's living room. She ignored Jeremiah's playful demands for attention from his high chair.

"What letters?" her mother asked confused by her daughter's fury.

"The letters from Jay. The letters he sent me. The letters you obviously hid from me!"

Her mother grew pale. She didn't want to have this conversation. She had hoped never to have it.

"Where are they Mom? Answer me!"

There was silence. Aliyah hoped she would deny their existence so she would have even more of an excuse to unleash her anger.

"How did you find out about them?" she quizzed, gathering her composure.

Wouldn't you love to know, Aliyah thought, her mind racing.

"Where are they?" she asked fiercely.

"I would imagine under tons of rubble at the county landfill by now," she said weakly.

"You had no right!" Aliyah exploded. "No right at all!"

Her mother frowned.

"Don't you raise your voice at me in *my* house," her mother rebuked, her own defenses awakening. "And I had every right. I am your mother. *I* carried you for nine months and suffered through fifteen hours of labor getting you into this world. *I* cleaned every wound, dried every tear, and caught every childhood disease nursing you back to health. *I* am the one who would take a bullet in my heart to protect you. I sacrificed my life for you."

The sun was starting to push its way through the morning clouds, lighting the attic and reminding Maya of how long she'd been up alone with her thoughts and the wall-to-wall discarded pieces of her short life story. Since the still quiet of midnight, she'd rummaged through boxes that carried her back in time ten years. Her mother had irritated her by demanding that she take all her "junk" with her when she moved in with Charles.

"You're a married woman now. Your things belong in your home," she said firmly.

She stretched hard, relieving each tired vertebrae

before pulling the last box off the shelf and opening the lid. A perfectly posed model on the cover of Life Magazine seductively stared back at her. Beneath that was her college graduation program and crumpled cap and gown. She dug through the box like a dog digging up a treasured bone, uncovering old Valentine's cards, faded term papers, and the tacky trinkets that had decorated her dorm room. And she found her address book, cracked and worn with dingy yellowing pages threatening to fall out with each slow, careful turn. It was filled with faded names that had seemed important in the chaotic madness of her twenties but that she now strained to remember. Except the one name she could never forget.

Jake T. Jackson

912-555-1244

Jake T. Jackson. That's how he'd written it in her book the night they met. As if he were already somebody important.

She didn't even remember asking him for his phone number, but he was so mesmerizingly gorgeous that she couldn't resist his command for her book and a pen. Jake was the kind of good looking everyone recognized. Even he knew he was handsome. Thick coal black waves of hair, dimples that were slightly visible even when he wasn't flashing a devilish smile, creamy skin, and deep eyes that drew you in to him and told beautiful lies like, "You're the only girl I've ever loved."

Jake T. Jackson. Triple traced and rewritten with a black marker.

"My friends call me J.T. Call me," he told her with a charm that made his demand sound more like a pleading request.

Calling was her first mistake among many.

For two hours she'd been trying to reach Jake, checking with friends and leaving messages at the fraternity house. She curled her aching body up into a knot, pleading with the doctor to wait and insisting she could take a few more hours of pain even though it felt like she was being stomped in the abdomen over and over again. When the bleeding started he refused.

"I'm not going to risk your life," he said, ordering her to surgery.

When she opened her eyes, the shooting pain she felt had become a dull ache. Jake was pacing the room, smelling like a nightclub mixture of perfume, sweat, and cigarette smoke.

"You should have told me you were pregnant," he said after realizing she was awake. They sat for a few minutes in silence with Maya hoping—needing—him to take her hand, kiss her, and tell her everything would be okay. Instead he said, "I guess this worked out for the best."

Maya had given Jake everything in exchange for nothing. The last time he walked out the door she couldn't mouth the word goodbye. She wanted to scream, "I hate you!" But she couldn't do that either. All she could do was cry.

Jake T. Jackson, a couple lines in a dusty old address book were all that remained of her first—maybe her only—real love affair. The photos of them together were burned in the kitchen sink over a bottle of cheap good riddance champagne. Every gift, card, or letter even remotely associated with him was thrown out the night she made up her mind to pick herself up and stop crying. He was gone and she emptied her life of every trace of him, except his page in her address book. She thought about tossing it right after the breakup, but there was no urgency. They had broken up before. He might call her. She might call him. Besides it wasn't as if she didn't know his number by heart. A year later she met Charles.

"I'm a practical man," Charles told her the night he proposed. "I have a good job, my own house, and a nice little nest egg I'm building for retirement. I'll be good to you," he said as he gave her an obligatory kiss.

Fifteen years her senior, Charles was a good man in his own way. Approaching forty, he was certain that if he didn't marry Maya he'd leave this earth with no children and no legacy to call his own. Love was an unnecessary bonus for a neurotic workaholic who feared the world would come crashing in on him at any moment and often secretly found comfort in a bottle of bourbon or vodka.

But saying yes to his proposal wasn't the hardest thing in the world. Maya told herself that eventually she could love him as she searched his eyes, held his hand, and occasionally hugged him too tightly hoping to feel something other than just contentment. Still she couldn't erase the fantasy of a fairytale ending to a love story that despite all of its problems was real—at least for her. And so she kept the address book tucked away quietly in her purse.

"Charles is decent and kind and smart . . . ," Maya's mother gushed to the chattering bridesmaids who stood around Maya nodding in synchronized agreement as if she needed reassurances. And maybe she did. She stood at the altar only half-listening to the pastor, watching and waiting instead for Jake. She'd sent him a wedding invitation, trying to fool herself and God that it was merely for closure. But really it was a test. If Jake had loved her at all he'd try to stop another man from having her. She rehearsed what she'd say when he burst through the church doors pleading with her to forgive him and to run away with him to some non-existent paradise.

"Will you have this man to be your lawfully wedded husband?" the Pastor asked, interrupting her thoughts. She took a deep breath, smiled, and said, "I do."

Charles didn't want anything cluttering his house. He groaned in disapproval when her boxes started arriving and ushered them into the stale darkness of the attic. He wanted her to throw everything out that didn't represent their new life together or fit into the few spaces he'd allocated for her. Maybe she would have if that horrible night hadn't happened.

The china cabinet hit the floor and an explosion of glass sprayed through the dining room. Set on an unstoppable rage started by a simple request to let the toilet seat down and fueled by a night of drinking, Charles roared, "Get out of my face!" He shoved her out of the house, tossing her purse and keys to the ground. "Go! I don't need you!"

Maya walked the block in a daze. She didn't even remember hopping onto the Number 12 downtown loop when she looked up to find herself sandwiched between tired late night commuters who were either headed home or to their cars that had been left alone all day at a Park 'n' Ride lot. She closed her eyes trying to hold in the tears, and rode until the driver called, "Last stop Riverfront."

She sat on the park bench under the watchful eye of the moon, following the gentle waves of the river and finally letting the tears flow until there was nothing left. Alone, depressed, and deflated, she found a payphone and thought about calling her mother. But what would be the point. She'd just give her a recipe for a casserole that would magically solve everything. "If you cooked better meals he'd be happier and drink less," she told Maya the first time she complained about Charles's drinking. For whatever reason, the only other person she could think to call was Jake.

She pulled the address book out of her purse and nervously dialed his number, half-heartedly praying that he wouldn't answer. It had been two years since they'd spoken or rather screamed at each other. On the third ring she started to hang up, but then she heard his unmistakable east coast swagger of a voice say, "Talk to me." She held her breath, listening and inhaling each hello until he grew tired of trying to prompt a response. Then oddly, for a few seconds he held the phone silently. His breath was steady and calming. Did he feel her on the other end of the line? Did he know she needed to hear him—to feel him with her in some strange way? She could have sworn she heard him softly say, "I love you" before he finally hung up.

Maya probably should have left Charles that night. Or the night the kitchen chair went flying across the room. Or after he punched the hole in the wall. Or after his hand stopped just inches from her face before he fell to the floor wailing an apology. But she didn't. She stayed with him. Sometimes out of pity because he was always trying—trying to have just one drink, trying to be a better man, trying to love her, and trying to make her love him. Mostly she stayed for the children who had arrived a little sooner than she had planned. Whenever she thought about leaving, a faint voice would always whisper to her spirit that staying was the right thing to do. So she stayed and she kept the address book close by.

Jake T. Jackson. She stared at the name and number that had finally made their way to a box in a dark corner of the attic a few years earlier—the same year Charles went to alcoholics anonymous for the first time and she found out she was pregnant with twins.

Maya closed the address book and put it in a large garbage bag filled with meaningless clutter and other relics of her past. The weight of the bag exhausted her as she dragged it down the steps and outside onto the curb with the rest of the waiting pile. She waved at the garbage man as he inched closer to her house before coming to a full stop.

"Good morning Miss Maya," he said in between whistles of a gospel tune she recognized. "How's Pastor doing today?"

"Better," she said. "Yesterday was his last treatment and his scans looked great."

"God is good!"

"Yes He is." But He has a strange sense of humor, she thought. Three years clean and sober, Charles finds Jesus, and takes over his father's role as minister in one of historic churches in town only to get sidelined by cancer.

She watched as the garbage man loaded each of her bags onto his truck, drove away, and turned the corner for his next pick up. It was done. Jake was gone.

Back inside the house, the shades were still drawn. It was 6:30 am. Aliyah and her brother would be downstairs in another hour looking for their Saturday morning pancakes shaped like Mickey Mouse. She and Charles decided weeks earlier that they were too young to be told what was happening.

The tea she'd started was ready. She poured two cups

and added honey and a twist of orange just as Charles liked it. She eased onto the couch beside him. A weak but welcoming smile came across his face as she rubbed the soft wisps of hair that were starting to grow back. She wrapped her hand around his thin fingers, helping him hold the cup to his lips. "I'm sorry to be such a bother," he said quietly.

In the seven years they'd been married, "I'm sorry" had echoed through each room, accompanied by flowers, candy, or some other token of repentance. Maya couldn't remember if she'd ever spoken those words to him, and it didn't matter. None of it mattered. She would keep her promise to God. The promise she made after the doctor said "cancer" and "fifty-fifty chance."

"If you let him live God, I promise to give myself to him completely," she kneeled and prayed that night in her bedroom closet, fighting back tears. It was strange, but at that moment she knew she cared for him, even loved him. Not like Jake, but loved him all the same.

"I never asked you to sacrifice for me," Aliyah said, her voice lowering with cold anger.

"Being a mother means sacrifice."

Her mother's voice was steady and sharp. Unapologetic. Aliyah couldn't know that every choice she made, including staying with their father, was for her and her brother. She hadn't worn her sacrifices with pride or self-righteousness. She did what she needed to do. She chose to do the right thing.

Jeremiah was crying now. Aliyah couldn't bring herself to pick him up. She didn't want to hear his cries. She wasn't even sure she wanted him to exist. Her mother hung him across her shoulder, rocking him and gently patting him on the back.

"You know, instead of walking around coveting the past, you should stop and thank God for all the blessings He's given you. You have a beautiful baby, a nice home, good health, and a husband who may not be perfect, but he's a good man and loves you."

Aliyah's jaw tightened. What did her mother know about love?

"Every choice I made may not have been right. But I did everything I did because I love you," her mother added as she worked to console Jeremiah. "And if I thought for one minute I could spare you a lifetime of pain, I'd do it all again."

Spare me pain. Can't you see my pain? Aliyah wanted to scream. Instead, she grabbed her purse and headed to the door.

"Where are you going?" her mother demanded.

"Out."

"What about Jeremiah?"

Aliyah stopped and looked at her son cradled in her mother's arms. "You're the great sacrificial lamb, not me," she said as she turned and slammed the door.

Maya stood in the doorway dumbfounded when Jay showed up unannounced and pleading to see Aliyah. His eyes were bloodshot and his clothes, although expensive, looked disheveled. He wasn't drunk, but he'd had a long night, the kind she never wanted Aliyah to experience. In a few days he would be leaving for Europe on a three-month tour. There were things he said he needed to tell her—things he was afraid she would see in the press and only know the half-truth. He knew she had to know about the baby, but he wanted to tell her it was an accident and that he still only wanted her.

After months of intercepting letters and telephone calls, it never dawned on her that he would show up at the house. She and Charles had never made an attempt to make him feel welcome in their home and now that he was becoming a superstar she hoped Chestnut Falls, minus any mention of Aliyah, was just a blip on his bio.

She had worked hard to secure the Reverend for Aliyah. A graduate of Princeton Theological Seminary and honor student, he stood dutifully at her husband's side building up the church. Aliyah had rolled her eyes and called him her father's gofer when they were first introduced. Now she was finally seeing his kindness and faithfulness. Even she was shocked by the suddenness of their engagement, but she didn't care. With the Reverend great things were possible and she would not allow Jay to swing in like a wrecking ball. She'd already had to make up a nonsensical excuse for Aliyah's sudden bolt from *the room one night when the Reverend was visiting. Jay appeared on a television award show on the arms of a woman with hair teased six inches above her head and clearly pregnant.*

"Aliyah isn't here," she finally told him. "She's getting fitted . . . for her wedding dress."

Her words pierced him like the violent sting of a bee on exposed flesh—quick, painful, and unexpected. He locked his fingers and rested his hands on his head and paced back and forth on the porch, trying to wish this moment away.

"I guess there's no point in coming back later," he said, his voice sullen and defeated.

"I'd say not."

"Can you just tell her that I came by and . . . that I love her?"

"If you really love my daughter, you'll do what I intend to do: pretend you were never here," she said, before shutting the door.

Maya sank into the sofa, holding Jeremiah. He was dozing off to sleep, his crying reduced to sporadic whimpers. She rocked him softly, feeling her own eyes welling up with tears. *Lord if I was wrong, please forgive me,* she prayed quietly, clinging to her grandson.

Chapter 14

Connie was becoming convinced God must be asleep at the wheel. Here she was one of the biggest frauds to proclaim His name and FLS embraced her. Lena was the real deal and was being rejected. She tried calling again, but there was still no answer. Poor Lena, she'd worked hard and her husband had messed things up. *Typical,* Connie thought as she opened a bottle of rum and coupled it with some warm soda that was stashed under her dressing table. She tossed it back and mixed another.

Studying her undone face in the mirror she traced the signs that age had been unkind, transforming her more and more into her mother. The older she got, the more Connie thought about her, the mother she'd hated as a child. Her daily drunken escapades—dancing in the street, climbing trees and pretending to be a superhero, or crashing her car into the garage—were always the morning talk of the otherwise quiet neighborhood. She wouldn't stop until she passed out in the yard, leaving Connie struggling to pull her lifeless body into the house.

"If she loved me, she'd stop," she'd sobbed to her father, the few times he bothered to come home before bedtime.

Her child's mind couldn't understand how life could push someone into self-destruction. As an adult she knew all too well and she wished she could embrace the mother she'd judged so harshly and who died too soon.

This year, her own child would have been twenty-one. Connie remembered every birthday and thought of the thousands of cuts and scrapes that would have been made better by a mother's kiss, the heartbreaks eased over a bowl of late night ice cream. She thought of how she might have stood with the other mothers, teary-eyed and proud watching their children march across the graduation stage in their caps and gowns. The Bishop never talked about their child, not since learning that there no longer was a child. She wondered if he really believed she'd miscarried. She suspected he knew the truth and wanted to put it out of his mind the way she planned to on this anniversary with the bottle of scotch she had cradled under her arm.

She downed her usual pre-broadcast drink and read over her scripted prayer. Her life was a joke in the most tragic sense. She took another drink, intending to stop with two. Two turned into three and then four, before the room became foggy. She barely made out the producer's voice calling her out of her dressing room.

"Sister Connie, Sister Connie, thirty seconds. Hurry!" he frantically pleaded.

Connie found the door and staggered to her mark on stage just as the curtains were opening. The bright lights stung her eyes and the roar of the crowd would have toppled her over if the Bishop hadn't been firmly gripping her arm. He could smell the liquor and he tightened his hold on her as they walked to their seats. Connie sat, slightly rocking, her glazed eyes trying to focus.

"Brothers and Sisters, the spirit of God is telling me the enemy is in here today," the Bishop said in a booming voice, cueing the cameraman in his direction. "Before we do anything else today, I want all eyes closed and every head bowed as we go to God in prayer to rebuke this demon."

The audience diligently obeyed. The lights were dimmed as the band played softly. The Bishop spoke powerfully into his microphone, commanding the devil to come out of hiding while shoving Connie behind the curtain and into the arms of his waiting assistant.

"Deal with this!" he mouthed to her as his piercing eyes raged. He moved toward the center of the stage and twirled his index finger in the air, signaling the band to get louder and faster.

"The devil has no power in here!" he shouted, while walking through the audience touching them on the forehead at random and sending most to the floor in tears.

Behind the thick velvet curtains, the Bishop's assistant tugged at Connie, trying to lead her back to her dressing room.

"Let me help you, Sister Connie," she said. Connie jerked away, breaking her fall by holding on to the wall.

"Get your hands off me," she said, her words running together. "I know what's going on with you and my husband. You want to replace me? You'll never replace me."

Connie flung open the emergency exit door and stumbled through the parking lot looking for her car. A beaming light headed toward her. God had finally come she thought and threw open her arms welcoming Him. The last thing she heard was a series of screams as her body hit the cold asphalt.

A swarm of mosquitoes circled around Lena, dotting in and out, plotting where to land to avoid being swatted. She had forgotten how bad they were in the country, especially at dusk. She had killed half a dozen since she'd come out onto her mother's porch. But waging war with them was the only thing reminding her that she was alive. When she walked out on Pastor, she was numb. That numbness was the only way she was able to ignore his pleas to stay. That numbness was all that kept her from falling apart.

"Sitting on this porch watching the sky won't solve your problems," her mother said, standing over her with a glass of homemade lemonade. She didn't feel like hearing a lecture, but she was thankful for the lemonade. It was one of the few things her growing unborn child would let her keep down. She'd thought about telling Richard about the baby before she left him, but decided against telling anyone, even her mother, until God guided her in what to do.

"I've been praying," Lena said wearily. "I prayed when the sun came up. I prayed while it was going down. God still hasn't answered me."

"Maybe He has and you just aren't listening."

Lena swung her legs to get the long, bench-like swing going again. She still couldn't believe her mother had a house on the lake. Three bedrooms, two bathrooms, and a half-acre of land, compliments of Stan's will. Even in death, he made sure her mother was still in his house.

Her mother sat beside her, steadying the swing. She didn't say much when Lena interrupted her morning coffee and told her about the Pastor. She just nodded and listened like a priest in a confessional booth. She'd left Lena alone all day with her thoughts; but, now, as they rocked, she took Lena's hand and squeezed it firmly as she had so many times when her little girl would come home crying after being teased about her green eyes, kinky blond hair, or any of the other differences the neighborhood children used to taunt and punish her. Back then all it took was her mother's strong hand wrapped around hers, leading her to a cup of warm bread pudding to dry up her tears. *If life were only that simple again*, Lena thought as she watched the last rays of sunlight duck down behind the clouds.

"Richard is a good man; he just made a mistake," her mother said gently.

"He did more than make a mistake," Lena objected. "He lied to me. He lied to everybody."

"I know, but baby you have to realize people and love aren't perfect."

Lena didn't expect her mother to understand. "I'm not like you," she huffed.

Lena had spent her life dreaming of a happily ever after fairytale. Her mother knew no such thing existed. She should have told Lena the truth when she was a little girl—that love is often painful. She should have told her more about Stan. But what could she say?

"I wanted to spend the rest of my life with you, not with the entire Negro race," Stanley said as he pulled his suitcase from the closet. His youthful, idealistic view *of love seemed childish now as he looked out onto the streets of a grayish city he hated; spending every night eating food and listening to music he had grown tired of; working in silence while the black men at the steel yard grumbled about the "oppressive white devil" always just loud enough for him to hear. He hated closing his eyes to make love to Eleanor and feeling like a million black faces were watching and scowling. He feared that if he didn't leave, he'd eventually end up hating her too.*

Life used to be simple. Under the stoic peace of his childhood, black hands fixed his favorite grilled cheese sandwiches, rocked him to sleep, and nursed his boyhood wounds. No one discussed the fact that the person attached to those hands couldn't share a swimming pool, water fountain, or cup of coffee at a downtown lunch counter with Stanley or his family. Things were the way they were, and people were happy until students with names like Schultz and Weinstein invaded Stanley's fine southern university and told them otherwise.

Appalled by the separate but equal state of things, Stanley's roommate dragged him to his first student organizing meeting inside a wood frame Baptist church he was sure he'd driven by a million times but had never had a reason to go inside. A few other white students were there, shuffling from one small group to another and making nervous conversation. Surrounded by broad noses and wide grins stretched across rich coffee and caramel skin, he felt particularly plain.

The meeting opened with a fiery prayer that ebbed and flowed poetically then peaked on cue of the music. Tambourines and an organ raced to keep up with the synchronized hums and heavy foot stomps that grew stronger and faster, leading people into a mesmerizing dance until thunderous calls for Jesus took over. Stanley sat entranced, studying the strong but suffering faces that had been no more than nameless shadows to him.

After singing and shouting themselves into exhaustion, the music stopped as dramatically as it had started. As if their power source had just been instantly shut off, they robotically sat in their seats, fanned themselves, and waited for the night's speaker to appear. And that's when he first saw Eleanor.

A high-energy, sandy-haired woman with delicate freckles who he thought was Jewish, maybe Puerto Rican until someone whispered, "I think she's colored." Whatever she was, she was beautiful. Noticeably the only female in the group of dark suited men, she confidently took the lead in directing the speaker to the microphone and arranged a set of papers in front of him before he began to speak. She stood dutifully by his side, nodding, frowning, and prompting the crowd to clap in all the right places. When he was finished, he handed the microphone to her.

The organ began creeping up from the background. "Are you with us?" Eleanor asked. "Yes!" the crowd yelled as the organ lurched forward, inviting a drum and guitar to join in. There was no singing this time. Just chants of "Yes! Yes! Yes!"

With the music still ringing in his head, Stanley scribbled his name down to go door-to-door in the Mississippi Delta and register blacks to vote. Eleanor gave him a quick approving smile.

"We leave in two weeks," she told him. "That gives you two weeks to change your mind."

And Stanley's father did everything in his power to get him to change his mind. "Are you crazy?" he exploded. "Mississippi is no place to fool around! You go running around with the Negros down there and you won't just get a beating, you'll get yourself killed."

"It's just for a few weeks," Stanley tried in vain to explain, not wanting to admit that he hadn't taken time to think anything through.

He urged Stanley to join the Peace Corps to satisfy whatever fool mission his "communist" friends had sent him on. Stanley refused and his father refused to give him money for the trip. Stanley decided to go anyway.

Under the guise of being missionaries, they would travel in groups of three covering a sixty-mile radius. Always two white people per group, which made some of the black students grumble in disapproval.

"We're going to give our people the power of the vote. It doesn't matter who gets it done as long as it gets done," Eleanor chastised. "The new guy can go with us," she said, pointing to Stanley.

The ride down was long, hot, and reflective. Their instructions were clear. They were to get in, get people registered, and get out. Local members of the Movement would take things from there. They were given a phone number to call if they found themselves in serious danger. No name, just a number, and the assurance that there were people in high places dedicated to ensuring their safety. But no one wanted to speak or think about the fact that they might have to flee for their lives in the middle of the night.

They took turns driving. They ate, slept, and read— Eleanor opening her Bible and Stanley with his first look at an Ebony magazine. Stanley was glad he was riding with Eleanor partly because she brought greasy brown bags of fried chicken, country ham biscuits, and mason jars filled with lemonade.

"There won't be a lot of places for us to stop," she said as she handed them their first rations. "At least not with me in the car with you."

Once in Mississippi they spent their time strategizing over bowls of pinto beans and cornbread any hosting family was gracious and brave enough to share under the protective covering of the night sky. They all liked Eleanor. She moved comfortably among the rows of barely standing shotgun houses, helping the women with laundry and combing the heads of the shoeless children milling about the black and white strangers who had come to liberate them.

"She'd make a good wife," Stanley said to himself almost embarrassed by the thought. He already knew she was much more than the blissfully oblivious housewives he'd grown up watching.

For two weeks, the sun preyed on them as they trounced through cotton fields and swamp-covered rice patties trying to convince workers that the good state of Mississippi couldn't keep them from voting. Eleanor usually did most of the talking while Stanley's eyes followed the stream of sweat running down the back of her sundress as she passionately talked about the brave new world that was coming. Some days they'd get as many as two new registered voters. Mostly they were acknowledged by no more than a quick non-committal nod that silently pleaded with them to go away.

With only a handful of voters to turn in, Stanley considered the trip a failure. But Eleanor wasn't deterred. "We're just getting started," she said. She had been watching Stanley since that first night in the church. His sharp green eyes caught her attention. They were alive, bright, and caring. They were beginning to be opened and see the things that were around him. She liked that he wasn't completely sure of himself and thought he was cute in an unassuming white guy kind of way. His sweat-soaked hair standing up like a porcupine was shockingly blond next to his burnt brick-red skin. When he talked, she noticed that his pink lips were fuller than most white people she knew and he didn't smell like a wet dog the way her father swore all white people did.

"Promise you won't quit," she said.

Silence.

"Promise," she demanded, nudging him playfully in the ribs.

"Okay, okay!" he laughed. "I promise."

But Stanley was relieved when they got home and the leader told them there would be no more trips down South . . . for now. There was work to be done at home.

"He's trying to get Dr. King to come back here and lead a march," Eleanor whispered to Stanley during a meeting. "There's talk the Mayor might meet with us."

They had to drive media attention to their city and the best way to do that was to target the infamously segregated downtown lunch counters. They rolled out an admirable plan that Stanley privately thought was as destined to fail as the voter registration drive in Mississippi. Still he had promised Eleanor he wouldn't quit, and he enjoyed spending more time with her, if for nothing more than to grab hold of her laughter that seemed to dissolve any feelings of hopelessness and doubt.

Discreet glances passed between them during sit-in training where they learned to be spit on and have insults hurled at them without reaction. They practiced how not to resist arrest and to effectively shield themselves from blistering water hoses and flesh-loving police dogs. They hovered around the radio, listening to Dr. King bellow his dream for the nation from the steps of the Lincoln Memorial and shared a candle and each other's grief over *the four lives forever lost to a bomber in Birmingham, Alabama. They locked hands at a prayer vigil for President Kennedy's family. Visions of his lifeless body slumped over a blood-stained first lady woke up the country and even Stanley couldn't imagine falling back to sleep.*

They raised paper cups filled with fruit punch and toasted President Johnson's signing of the Civil Rights Act. That night they all laughed and danced, Eleanor teaching Stanley to move his lean square hips to the beat of Martha and the Vandellas. He tried to teach her to smoke a cigarette. She instead convinced him it wasn't a habit worth learning or keeping.

Whenever they had a chance to be alone, they talked. Stanley learned that Eleanor's mother, who was part Irish but had refused to talk about it, died when Eleanor was thirteen years old. They had traveled all over the country in a beat up van with a band of like-minded explorers. The world was her classroom. Her mother believed that everybody loved something, even if it was no more than loving to hate. The secret, she told a girlish Eleanor, was to tap into that capacity to love. A smile took over her whole face when she talked about traveling to Africa one day to teach and build houses for the poor. That had been her mother's dream before her death "sentenced" Eleanor to the south to live with a father she'd really only known through photographs. Her father loved her. She knew that. But she also knew he wished she looked like her legitimate brothers and sisters as if he wasn't the one who made the choice to lay under a willow tree one cool autumn night with her "high yella" mother.

"Sometimes I wish I looked like everybody else," she confessed one night as they cleaned up the church. Her massive curls were pulled back in a headband with a few escaping and accenting her soft and thoughtful face. As strong and smart as she was, there was a vulnerability she wasn't afraid to show.

"I think you're beautiful," Stanley said unexpectedly. He dropped his eyes to the floor like a shy, pubescent schoolboy caught staring at his first crush. Eleanor's cheeks turned a deep crimson as she smiled and restacked hymnals that were already perfectly placed.

"So why did you join the Movement?" she asked him, quickly trying to change the subject. It was too late. The words Stanley had been trying to find a way to say for months were finally out there, hanging in the air.

"I don't know. I guess I want to be on the right side of history," he answered. He moved closer to her, so close that he could feel her breath on his face. He had never been this close to a black woman before—not in this way.

"Maybe I want to be on the right side of you," he said before giving her a short kiss on the cheek, deliberately catching the corner of her mouth. When she didn't resist, he held her face gently in his hands and let their lips melt into each other.

Three weeks later they quietly and illegally eloped in Memphis. Eleanor pretended to be white so they could stay at one of the downtown hotels for their one-night honeymoon.

She was nervous and surprisingly so was he. He had been with his share of giggling white sorority girls, but never a black woman. She slipped into bed, just barely letting him get a peek at her in her nightgown. Her warm thighs touched his. He caressed her back and ran his hand along the side of her leg and lifted the hem of her gown. As their bodies pressed together he could feel her heart racing. Soon he knew he was the only man she'd ever been with.

When they came home there were no celebrations.

"As long as you're with that girl, your life is over," his father said, shutting the door while his mother stood at the window weeping. He hadn't imagined that his father might be right.

Conduct unbecoming was the reason given for his expulsion from school. It didn't take long to realize there were no good jobs for a "nigger lover." Eleanor tried to stay active in the Movement but gave up after she was told by more than a few that her "situation" had "complicated things." And no one would rent to them.

Eleanor's father begrudgingly let them move in with him only to chastise Eleanor for being a silly dreamer just like her mother. "You two are lucky you ain't in jail or worse," he said irritably. He quizzed Stanley about his plans after his infatuation with his French-vanilla-skinned daughter was done. Stanley assured him he would never leave her side.

"Stupid, stupid, stupid," they heard every night through the walls.

Her father's tolerance ended the day his supervisor called him into the office to inform him that he was "dismissed until further notice." He gave them fifty dollars and two train tickets to Chicago to stay with Eleanor's aunt and uncle.

"There'll be a job and an apartment waiting for you when you get there," he said.

"I can provide for my own wife," Stanley insisted.

"And ain't you doing a fine job of that so far," Eleanor's father said, shooting him a look that dared Stanley to say one more word.

So they packed their bags and told themselves that they'd be fine as long as they had each other. Northern stares weren't the same as southern ones, but they were stares all the same. Stares from Jack the big Jamaican that warned, "I'm gonna take dat gal from ya one day," or Abbie, a part-time member of the black power group when it suited her, who watched their comings and goings from behind floral velvet curtains and gossiped that they were sent in by the FBI to infiltrate the neighborhood. Nell the cook and Bernie the barber gave them polite good mornings and good evenings, but stopped short of inviting them to the Friday night fish fries or rent parties. Those involved in the Movement were different too. They seemed more interested in the fire of a man named Malcolm than the unifying olive branch of Dr. King. When

Malcolm was killed everybody on the block watched Stanley suspiciously and whispered how lucky he was that a white man didn't do it, reminding him that his life was in their hands.

Their social circle was mainly Eleanor's aunt and uncle. Monday through Friday was work. Saturdays offered cards over pizza and Coca-Cola. A few times Eleanor's uncle took him to the bowling alley with his league partners, but that mostly only made everyone feel uncomfortable. On Sundays they went to church, usually without Stanley, and Eleanor and her aunt would spend the rest of the afternoon cooking while Stanley and her uncle silently stared at the television screen.

After three long years, life for them hadn't become easier. Stanley wanted to go home. He wanted to wade his feet in the lake on a humid summer afternoon, eat roasted peanuts at the county fair, and get drunk off cheap watery beer by a bonfire after a high school football game. He wanted to open Christmas presents with his parents under the crooked, dying tree his father always got for half price on Christmas Eve. He was ashamed to admit it, but he wanted to feel like a white man again—entitled, powerful, and in control.

"I wanted to spend the rest of my life with you, not the entire Negro race," he rehearsed again in the mirror. Eleanor wouldn't come with him. She couldn't. She'd be better off and happier with a black man. Technically they weren't even legally married anyway, he tried to convince

himself. Suddenly his thoughts were interrupted as Eleanor frantically burst into the apartment screaming.

"Stanley, he's dead! He's dead!" she cried out. Stanley raced into the living room. Her whole body was trembling as she fell into his arms.

"Calm down. Who's dead? What's going on?" he asked.

"Dr. King . . . he's . . . dead . . . they . . . killed him," she said trying to take in gulps of air between each word and her sobs. Stanley carried her to the bedroom and placed her limp body on the bed. Feeling his own legs about to give out from under him, he moved his empty suitcase to the floor. She buried her face in his chest. All he could do was let her cry for the both of them.

Hours passed. Thick heavy clouds hung low over the city. The sound of police sirens grew stronger from the distance. By now, everyone knew the dreamer was dead. Sadness was turning to rage over the evil darkness that had suffocated the last remaining light of hope. What would happen now? Too many had come too far to turn back. But who would carry them into the Promised Land? Stanley wasn't even sure such a place existed anymore.

She looked up to face him, her eyes swollen, bloodshot, and tired. She's still beautiful, Stanley thought as she pressed her forehead against his.

"What will we do?" Eleanor asked weakly. She took his hand and placed it on her soft extended belly. Today was supposed to be a good news day. Heaven had already grabbed two babies from her womb, their heartbeats prematurely stopped. This time she'd waited as long as she could to tell Stanley. "What will we do with this baby?"

A baby. What would they do with a mixed up half black, half white, half Irish, and whatever else baby in a world that had been turned upside down? Eleanor was supposed to have the answers. She always did during these times. She was the believer. Stanley had long come to realize that white man's guilt was all he'd set out to conquer. In the comfort of his middle-class suburban retreat, he would have reminisced about how he had helped "those people." Running his fingers through thinning gray hair, he could have pulled out pictures of himself on picket lines and sharing a pack of cigarettes in a jail cell as proof that he used to be young and cool. Over a dry martini and cigar he would have boasted to his son—out of earshot of his wife—that he had once kissed a black woman.

If a kiss had only stayed a kiss . . . things would have been much easier.

Eleanor was drifting to sleep. Her crying had turned to sporadic sniffles and he gently stroked her hair. What would they do with a baby?

"Love it," Stanley finally said, holding Eleanor tighter and trying to reassure her, but knowing he'd be gone in the morning.

"When your Daddy and I met we thought we could conquer the world," she said, not looking at Lena. "We didn't expect the world to conquer us."

She missed Stan and Lena hated the sad weakness in her mother's voice. She hated herself even more. She was a grown woman who still would have given anything just to hear him call her his little girl. She wondered if he would have if he'd seen her that night she stood silently in the corner of his hospital room.

Even with the angel of death and eternal judgment clasping its hand around his throat, Stan was afraid to face his shame uncovered by the moonlight. Hiding in the shadows had become Lena's birthright.

The antiseptic and deserted hallways of the hospital extended endlessly, taking her through an identical maze of ramps, nurses' stations, and private waiting rooms that had become nightly campsites for the praying faithful and mournful realists.

She was careful to make sure her mother was gone. There was no point in trying to make this a family reunion. Once in Stan's room, she tiptoed as close as she could to him without waking him. But she could tell that he was as good as dead except for the air being pumped into him by machines. She studied his face and saw her own. They shared the same nose, the same mouth, and the same sharp cheekbones. Even though they were closed tightly, she remembered the green eyes she'd inherited.

"I loved your Daddy, he loved me, and whether you want to believe it or not, he loved you," her mother said as if reading her thoughts.

"How can I ever forgive Richard?" Lena asked, not wanting to think about her father anymore.

"If you really love him you'll find a way, especially for the sake of my grandbaby." Her mother gave her a knowing and compassionate smile and patted her slightly pooched stomach.

The house was dark and lonely. The dishes were where Lena had left them and a rank odor filled the kitchen. There were twenty messages waiting on the answering machine and she thought she was alone until she heard Richard racing down the steps. He stopped when he saw her and waited for her to invite an embrace. She walked over to the sofa, sat rigidly on the edge, and placed her purse on the coffee table. The house didn't look or feel the same. Everything was different. She almost wished for the lie again as he sat beside her trying pathetically to hold her hand.

For the first time, he didn't know what to say or how to make things right.

"Tell me what you want," he pleaded as he searched for signs of the love that had so vividly danced in her eyes each time he entered the room before he had imploded their world.

"A lot," she said sharply. She wanted a partner, respect, a voice in their marriage. She wanted to have fun. She wanted to trust again."But we'll start with you telling the church what you've done."

"Tell the church?" Lena's indignation had jolted him. "They might throw us out. I might never preach again."

"If we're going to stay together those are my terms. I'm not going to spend my life looking over my shoulder worried about somebody finding out about our dirty little secret," she said, unwavering.

"I could go to jail," he tried to reason.

Lena didn't care about leaving the church. Somehow it was the church that had made them take their focus off God. She hadn't thought about the possibility of him going to jail, but that might be the price of true freedom. Maybe God still had an ounce of mercy left for them.

"Those are my terms. You can do the right thing and stay or keep lying and leave, but I'd rather not have our child sitting by the window longing for a father to show up like I did."

Richard's eyes met hers, questioning without words. She let him touch her stomach. He put his arms around her and began to sob uncontrollably.

"Tell me you still love me. Please, tell me you still love me," he pleaded.

"I do love you," she said, her voice weak and tired. She relaxed a bit and eased back into the sofa.

"Will you stand with me before the church?" he asked, finally accepting his defeat.

Lena reached for her purse and placed a folded check in his hand as he dropped to his knees in front of her. For the first time since they'd been together, he looked small and fragile, like he needed her. She pulled him close to her. His head rested on her stomach as he cried.

"What's this?" he asked.

"Redemption," she said with a sigh.

Her mother had surprised her with a copy of her father's will and a key to a safe deposit box. The check was less than half of what he'd actually left her in a bank account, but she decided Richard didn't need to know everything—not anymore. "You'll take this money and pay off your *friend* and then you *and* I will go to the church and confess what happened."

Chapter 15

Aliyah adjusted her dress. The body shaping underwear was starting to pinch, but she'd liked how she looked in the mirror before she lied to the Reverend and said she was going out to dinner with some of the FLS women. She almost changed her mind about going when he looked at her, told her she looked good, and kissed her goodbye. But she was still angry with her mother.

The elevator ride to the secluded presidential suite of the hotel was long and reflective. She punched in the access code Jay had given her and stood holding her breath alone in the elevator as the doors opened, Down the hallway stood a bodyguard, keeping watch in front of Jay's door. His eyes followed Aliyah as she came closer.

"Jay's expecting me," she said timidly as she handed him Jay's letter.

The bodyguard looked suspiciously at the letter and ducked inside Jay's hotel room. Seconds later, Jay emerged with his arms spread wide and a large smile spanning his face. He was bare foot and dressed in a loose-fitting linen shirt and pants with the drawstring just visible under the hem of his shirt—a little more casual than Aliyah expected.

"Princess!" he said, throwing his arms around her and giving her a long, strong embrace.

English Leather. Jay was a multi-millionaire and still wore his favorite drugstore cologne. Just a hint on the back of his neck, the way she remembered.

"You look great," he said, pulling himself back to look at her. "If I weren't a saved man, you'd be in trouble," he laughed. He didn't ask about her husband or if he'd be joining them as he took her hand and lead her inside.

She was hit by a sweet delicate fragrance coming from two large crystal vases perched on the mantel. They were filled with pink and white star lily flowers and Aliyah wondered if the flowers were a coincidence or if Jay remembered they were her favorite.

A large white sofa lined the entire wall of the living room with a chaise at each end facing the fireplace. A marble statue of a half- dressed Greek goddess stood guard over a white piano. Aliyah noticed a large glass coffee table in the center of the room with a silver tray covered with an assortment of cheeses and fruits and what looked like a wine bottle. The room was illuminated by the night sky visible from a window the size of a movie theater screen that led to the balcony. Aliyah had never noticed how beautiful the skyline was at night. From the top floor of the hotel, the stars looked as clear as diamonds and she reached for the balcony door to get a closer look.

"Let's not do that," Jay said, grabbing her hand. He pushed a button on the wall and the blinds moved together and closed tightly. The ceiling opened gradually revealing a cluster of tiny lights mimicking the stars.

"Sorry about that, but somebody will be trying to climb the balcony or fly overhead if anybody suspects this is my room," Jay told her.

"You must have some loyal fans."

"They're not all fans. Some are just autograph hounds who auction off things with celebrity signatures. Others are paparazzi, and they're the worst. They'll do anything to get a picture, even pay moles to spy at local hotels. Clear window shots pay top dollar depending on the celebrity and what they are doing."

"Sounds rough. So what are you worth might I ask?"

"With a sold out tour, hit record, and newly professed faith in Christ, I hear a picture of me indulging in even one vice will get about $10,000. After today's appearance on CBTV, it's probably higher. Everybody wants to see me fall so they can put it on the cover of a magazine."

At that moment, Aliyah almost regretted wearing the backless, body-hugging dress she'd pulled from the back of her closet.

"But it's all good. It comes with the territory," he said, sensing her discomfort. "And you don't know how good it is to see you. I think you're getting some curves, aren't you?" he teased.

Aliyah grunted. Her curves were the last thing she wanted him to notice.

"It looks good on you," he reassured.

Before she could say anything, his telephone rang. He looked at his watch.

"I've got to take this call. I promised the local paper a telephone interview. Twenty minutes tops, I promise.

Jay went into the bedroom. Aliyah could hear his flirtatious laughter through the walls as he talked to the reporter. Must be a female. Stacks of fan mail lined the edge of the coffee table, along with some pictures of Jay posing next to a motorcycle wearing a leather jacket and no shirt. Just a hint of his rippled abs was visible. He'd started to sign a few, "To my beautiful Jaybird fan." The clutter looked a lot like her husband's desk.

She toyed with the idea of opening a few of the letters as she did with the perfumed envelopes she'd found under his dressing room door years ago. Jay was always quick to dismiss his female admirers as "nobody." But there had been indiscretions. He'd even confessed to one—a backup singer in New Jersey. She cried for weeks. He promised it would never happen again. It's funny how she'd forgotten about that. She changed her mind about opening anything and explored the living room. As big as the suite was, it didn't feel like a home, just a staged oversized hotel room. She nibbled on a strawberry and made a small sliver in the blinds with her finger.

She noticed about a dozen people standing coyly outside the hotel. Some were carrying cameras. She quickly moved away from the window when she heard Jay coming back into the room.

"No matter how hard I try to sneak in these hotels, *they* always find me," he said, smiling.

They sat on the sofa with a little distance between them, taking in the fact that they hadn't seen or talked to each other in three years. He poured her a drink.

"The best sparkling cider this side of the ocean," he laughed. "I gave up drinking a year ago," he explained.

"Well you've definitely come a long way, in more ways than one, since that studio apartment on 12th Street," she said.

"I owe it all to Him." He pointed a finger to the heavens.

"To God's goodness and mercy," she offered a toast, feeling like a hypocrite. She hadn't come there thinking about God.

"So I guess I should get you fed. There's a menu on the table. The kitchen is ours. Order whatever you want," he told her.

Aliyah had imagined candles, music, and a waiter catering to her every need. Maybe there'd be a limo ride. Not that Jay could know she hadn't been out to a nice restaurant in almost a year. He quickly noticed the look of disappointment on her face.

"Trust me, it's going to be a lot easier if we eat in. Besides what would people think if they saw a picture of you and me leaving a restaurant at night splashed across a grocery store tabloid?" he explained.

Jay was no longer anonymous and it had just occurred to her that neither was she. What could a picture like that mean for the Reverend? All she wanted to do was feel beautiful, desired, and visible again—all the ways Jay had made her feel once upon a time. Now she was feeling like she should leave, but there was a part of her that desperately wanted to stay.

The phone rang again and Jay excused himself. Aliyah thumbed through the menu suddenly not feeling as hungry. He was gone only a few minutes this time. When he sat back down on the sofa, he moved closer and Aliyah felt her heart thumping again against her chest.

"How is your little boy?" she asked suddenly, trying not to squirm. "I heard somewhere that you'd had a son." The vision of that night in the restaurant with the Reverend still etched in her mind along with the headlines the week of her wedding: *Music star and supermodel welcome their first child.*

"Not so little anymore. He's three going on thirty," he laughed.

"You and your . . . ," Aliyah wasn't sure if he'd told the truth about his status at the studio or if he was just teasing the women in the audience. A settled down sex symbol didn't sound as exciting. "You and his mother must be very proud."

"We are. I wish we'd done things the right way though. But it's cool. She has her life; I have mine, and we work together to do what's best for our little man."

She didn't know why, but she felt relieved. She'd lied to the Reverend about where she was going, and in some strange way she felt better knowing Jay didn't have to lie to anyone.

"The great thing about kids and God is they really do love us even when we're unlovable."

To the one who loved me when I was unlovable. Aliyah suddenly felt stupid and ashamed. All these years, she'd assumed—hoped—Jay had dedicated his albums to her. He'd clearly become deeper.

"Listen, uh, I want you to know he—my son—didn't come along until after we were over," he said. "Well I mean he was on the way, but I didn't know it and . . ."

"It's okay," she said, wanting to ease his embarrassment.

"I just want you to know I never stopped loving you," he admitted unexpectedly. "I meant what I said today on the show. When you dumped me and got married, it was a hard blow. But I deserved to be dumped, and if you hadn't done it I probably never would have gotten to know God and His love. I know that sounds crazy coming from a guy like me."

"No it doesn't," Aliyah said, trying to smile and not cry. "It sounds beautiful and I'm really happy for you Jay."

"I'm happy for you too," he said. "You've got a new baby right? And I hear you and that pastor husband of yours are headed for big things. I saw you in a magazine. Rising pastor of the year."

She nodded.

There was a brief moment of comfortable silence between them then Jay moved closer to her, took her hand, and kissed her palm softly just as he did the first night they met. He pulled her to him and held her, stroking her hair as her head rested on his shoulder, like he'd done so many years ago. Without thought, he lifted her lips to his just as the bodyguard from the hallway burst in.

"Sorry boss, but we've got to switch hotels! They've made you!" he said anxiously.

Startled, Lena pulled away, ashamed of where she'd allowed her mind to go. Jay looked apologetically at her as his bodyguard started collecting his things. Then the phone rang. It was Jay's publicist.

"I know, I know. I know the routine. Have someone handout a few free tickets and CDs while I'm sneaking out."

Jay and Aliyah stood looking at each other. There would be no dinner. There would probably be no seeing each other ever again. There were so many things left unsaid between them, but the most important thing had been said. They embraced one last time before being pulled apart by his staff that had come from out of nowhere and taken over the room. Aliyah was hustled to a service elevator as a man who looked eerily like Jay stepped off.

Outside, she wormed her way through the crowd that was now being held back by hotel security. "We love you J. Prince!" hundreds were yelling from the sidewalk. Some were even carrying signs, displaying their names and phone numbers. A far cry from the damp napkin she had slipped in his hand when they were both two very different people. Jay's decoy appeared on the balcony, waving and sending the screaming fans into a crying fit. He tossed out a few autographed CDs before disappearing behind the curtain.

Aliyah smiled to herself and finally let a few soft tears roll down her face. She realized life with Jay would have been different, not necessarily better. Aliyah had needed to know that Jay had loved her as much as she'd loved him. Her heart belonged to him, and the heart carries its secrets to the grave. But, her spirit had to let go. In her own way, Aliyah's mother had been right. She wouldn't admit it, but she would apologize . . . tomorrow.

Cinnamon toast. Aliyah smelled the fresh buttery sweetness before she opened her eyes. She took a few breaths and felt a soft hand run down the side of her cheek. Startled, she opened her eyes and sat up in bed. It was 10:00.

"I made you some breakfast."

The Reverend was sitting next to her holding a plate of toast and bacon. He'd placed a glass of orange juice on the nightstand.

"You got in so late last night, I thought I'd let you sleep in."

Her mouth was dry and she took a sip of the juice. She felt her stomach rumble and realized that she'd never had dinner. The bacon had burnt edges where the Reverend had left it in the skillet too long. But the toast was sweet and tender.

"Thank you," was all she could manage to say.

He studied her face, a look of distress covering his own. When Aliyah got home, he was already in bed. She didn't want to wake him or risk him detecting the smell of Jay's cologne, so she tipped into the guest room. She pretended not to hear him softly knock as she rolled over and went to sleep.

"I told the church to cancel all my calls today. I thought maybe we could go to that winery you've been talking about forever," he said, offering her a half smile. "I talked to your mom and she said she can watch Jeremiah a little while longer. Or we can do something else. Whatever you want. It's your day."

Aliyah put the plate down and shifted her weight, making more room for him on the bed.

Chapter 16

Connie pried one eye open at a time. They were heavy and dry. She wasn't dead. She was in too much pain. Her head felt like someone had beaten it with a hammer. The hospital room was coming into focus and she was able to make out the Bishop's face. He was sitting at the foot of her bed, his head cradled in his hands and his eyes closed. He was praying. Her squirming got his attention and she struggled to find her voice as he leaned in to give her a strained kiss.

"Don't try to talk," he said. "You gave us all quite a scare."

Connie surveyed the damage on the parts of her body that she could see. Her right arm was covered in a cast from her wrist to her shoulder. The tips of her fingers were swollen with layers of skin missing. She didn't want to see her face.

"Our phone has been ringing off the hook with well-wishers. The mayor, governor, just everybody," he said with an edge of excitement. "This even made the national news. We have requests for interviews from all the major television news magazines."

She had been awake for two minutes and already she wanted to go back to sleep.

"The man who hit you feels so bad. He was speeding, but I asked the DA not to press charges. I thought maybe we could have him on the show. He can apologize to you in front of thousands. Maybe he's a Christian, if not we can bring him to Christ. Imagine that; you sitting with the man who almost killed you and forgiving him. Wouldn't that be an amazing show? Anyway, I figured we should wait and do the first interview after you get out of the hospital, showing what a miraculous recovery you've made."

She listened to him ramble on and on.

"No," she finally managed to get out.

Her voice was raspy and almost unrecognizable to herself.

"Well your face is awfully bruised and I know you're self-conscious," he continued. "But maybe some make-up . . . "

"No," she said again. She couldn't remember the last time she'd said no to him. Judging from his reaction neither could he.

"I was drunk, David," she said clearing her throat.

"I know it, you know it, and everyone around us knows it. I won't pretend like this was some random, freak accident and I was an innocent victim."

He sat by her bed unsure of what to do next. "All right," he said, somewhat taken aback by her indignation. "Then we'll address it together. We'll tell the whole story about that night. The people will love you even more for your honesty. Everyone God uses has imperfections."

The *whole* story? They were both afraid of the *whole* story.

"No." Just saying the word again was making her feel better. "My imperfections are not a publicity campaign."

"This is for God," he tried to insist.

"David, we haven't done anything for God in a long time."

He rose from the bed and stood gazing out the window. Their life hadn't been so bad. He'd made a respectable woman out of her and given her a lifestyle she couldn't have imagined. He loved God. She couldn't question that, even if he had made some mistakes.

Connie hadn't meant to hurt his feelings. She cared for him, more than he probably ever cared for her. But she had been his salvation project long enough. It was time for her to save herself.

"I guess there's nothing else to talk about," he said sullenly.

There was plenty to talk about, but Connie wasn't in the mood.

"What should I tell our followers?"

"That I'm taking some time off to spend with God."

Lena snuck double-batter-dipped onion rings into Connie's hospital room. She and Aliyah had to pretend to be relatives the first time they came to see her. Now they were the only ones she allowed to visit. Today was her last day before she would be discharged and delivered by private jet to a spiritual rejuvenation resort. At least that's what their press release was calling the rehab center.

"I made them myself," she said proudly. The grease was bleeding through the paper sack. "I was going to make a beer batter, but in light of the circumstances . . ."

Connie laughed, causing her swollen ribs to jiggle. "Oh, that hurt."

"These are going to ruin my diet," Aliyah said, spreading some on a paper plate.

"I can eat your share since I'm eating for two now," Lena said, pausing for their reaction. It was the first time she'd announced it with some joy.

A broad grin stretched across Aliyah's face. "I thought you were getting some hips," she said.

"When my bones mend I'm going to throw you the best shower this city has ever seen," Connie declared. "Did you tell her?" she asked Aliyah, solemnly. Aliyah nodded sadly.

"I'm sorry about FLS. I know how much it meant to you."

"It's okay," Lena said. She took Connie's hand and Lena's making a small circle around the bed. "I wanted to be a part of something special and I'd say things worked out pretty good for me."

Connie squeezed their hands. She was glad they were with her. They were the daughter's she could have had if things had been different.

"Well, somebody get me some ketchup. If I'm going to clog up my arteries, I might as well go all out," she said maneuvering an onion ring toward her mouth with her one good arm.

Epilogue

They started coming to the pier last spring when the new flowers were blooming and the river moved gracefully downstream catching the sun. The beautifully graying couple found each other on Facebook and they were now sitting on the park bench, looking admiringly at each other. He made the two-hour trip once a month, bringing her chocolate even though she didn't need it. Occasionally she read him her poetry. Mostly they just talked—sometimes about important things and sometimes not.

Today they sat quietly and grieved. Maya's argument with Aliyah still weighing on her mind and Jake surrendering to the fact that the wife he didn't deserve wasn't coming back.

"The kids have decided it's time to clean out Elise's things," he said, expelling a defeated sigh.

Maya remembered the day he told her that his wife

knew him as nothing more than a stranger walking through the house. On a good day, she thought he was her father. He had surprised Maya by crying on her shoulder and then trying to kiss her.

"She's still alive and she's still your wife," Maya gently rebuked.

"You were always better than me," he said softly as he looked aimlessly out toward the river.

That was four months ago. The disease had taken her mind and life much quicker than anyone expected. There were two short-lived marriages before this one. The first, imposed on him for the sake of an unborn child—the product of a one-night stand. He knew he should have held Maya and found words to comfort and reassure her that night in the hospital after she miscarried. But all he felt was relief. He wouldn't have two women pregnant at the same time. Making her hate him completely was the hardest part, but it was the only way he could bear walking down the aisle with someone else.

"I'm just not digging you anymore," he said, making a point not to look at her.

By the time he discovered the child the other woman was carrying wasn't his, Maya was gone for good. The posed smile in the wedding announcement that showed up in the mail was unconvincing, but he had lost the right to try to make her love him again.

The second marriage happened over a bottle of

Vodka after a long night at a Las Vegas blackjack table. It lasted sixteen hours—just long enough for them to sober up and sign the annulment papers.

His last marriage to Elise was comfortable. She didn't ask for or expect more than he was capable of giving and accepted the presence of a nameless, invisible woman occupying his thoughts at times.

"You miss her don't you?" Maya asked.

"She was a good woman," he said solemnly.

Maya knew his grief. Understood it. She'd felt it when her own husband died. The loss of life could be overcome. The real grief was in knowing you'd spent a lifetime with someone without ever giving your whole heart even though it was deserved.

After his funeral, she climbed into bed, clutched the pillows from what had been his side and cried for two straight weeks. One morning she woke up startled by the rich woody scent of his cologne—the way he smelled when he had just gotten out of the shower—throughout the bedroom. She rolled over, thinking maybe she had been trapped in a dream. He would be lying beside her and she could make things right. He wasn't. But a still, faint voice inviting her to get out of bed and forgive herself said to her spirit, *We did all right.*

"You loved her and she knew it," Maya said, patting Jake's knee the way people do at that age. He placed his hand on top of hers.

Unlike most women her age, Maya didn't have to

try hard to look good. She had an understated beauty that Jake hadn't fully appreciated when they were younger—buttery skin brushed with a few lifelines, hair shining like freshly polished silver, and just a hint of red lipstick. She had become elegant in an approachable way.

As they held hands, Maya could see traces of the Jake from decades ago. Moving with the slowness that old age brings, his tall, athletic frame was still commanding. His coal black hair highlighted with streaks of gray showed only a slight trace of thinning on top if you looked closely. And his eyes, even hidden behind discreet bifocals, drew in everyone he talked to. The charming smile was still there too. Just not as devilish.

"What do you think it would have been like if we'd gotten married?" he asked.

"Gotten married to who?"

"Each other of course."

She curled her lips.

"A complete, utter disaster," she said without hesitation.

"You don't have to sound so convinced," he said, defensively.

"I'd be in prison right now for your murder or for cutting off your manly bits. Snip, snip!" she teased, motioning her hands like scissors.

Jake laughed, harder than expected. Releasing all of

his emotions in one long, loud burst—laughing over the foolish necessity of youth, over the joys, sorrows, and the everything in between of life. He laughed over the fact that he was a fifty-five-year old man feeling like a schoolboy sitting with his first crush—his first love.

"Thank you," he said, wiping his eyes with a handkerchief and regaining his composure.

"For what?" Maya asked, smiling.

"Just thank you."

He reached inside his jacket pocket and handed her a small box.

"I almost forgot to give you these."

Inside were three dark chocolates about the size of a silver dollar with the letter M masterfully swirled in the center.

"Specially made for you."

Maya popped one into her mouth and exhaled deeply, savoring the rich sweetness of the rum-tinged chocolate as it melted smoothly over her tongue. Jake watched her, delighted by the pleasure his small gift brought, and then he leaned in and gave her a soft easy kiss on the lips, the kind that wanted nothing but to be enjoyed.

THE END

About the Author

Rita Turner is a former journalist and attorney and holds a graduate certificate in Christian Education. Rita regularly speaks to women and youth about successful Christian living and includes anecdotes from her own faith journey. Rita is a ten-year victor over cancer who believes you should live every day inspired to be better. She has combined her love for God and great fiction in her first novel, *God's Daughters And Their Almost Happily Ever Afters*. She currently works in executive leadership and lives just outside Nashville, Tennessee with her husband and two sons.

CPSIA information can be obtained
at www.ICGtesting.com
Printed in the USA
LVHW032153041221
705303LV00001B/32

9 780996 499606